"I was thinking of making tiramisu, but ran out of time. Next time," he promised.

That caught her completely off guard.

"Next time?" she repeated, feeling as if the words were suddenly falling from her lips in cartoonlike slow motion.

"Yes. Unless you want to be the one to make the dessert," he told her.

Except for scrambled eggs and toast, she was a total disaster in the kitchen when it came to doing anything but cleaning it.

"I'd rather not have to call the paramedics," she told him.

His smile was nothing if not encouraging. "It can't be that bad."

"It's not that good, either," she told him.

It was supposed to be a flat, flippant denial but she just couldn't seem to get her head in gear because her mind was currently focused elsewhere.

It was focused on the way Eddie's lips moved when he spoke.

Tiffany rose to her feet, thinking that she would make a getaway, or at least make some sort of an excuse and slip into the bathroom, away from him. But he rose with her and suddenly she wasn't going anywhere.

At least not without her lips, and they were currently occupied. More specifically, they were pressing against his.

MATCHMAKING MAMAS: Playing Cupid. Arranging dates. What are mothers for?

Dear Reader,

The question I get most has always been "Where do you get your ideas?" With close to three hundred books to my name, that is more than a legitimate question. But after thirty-five years, my answer is still the same: everywhere. I cannibalize everything and anything—in a good way. As I observe life around me, things just have a way of suggesting themselves to me. When my two kids were little, and had so much energy they put the Energizer Bunny to shame, they were my inspiration for every kid that turned up in my books. It got to the point that my boisterous crew became suddenly silent around me, sharing nothing for fear of it turning up in one of my books.

But I didn't use just my kids, I used everything. Like a starving man wandering into an apple orchard, I feasted on everything: newspaper articles, TV programs, movies, songs (I wrote three books while playing Eddie Rabbitt's *Every Which Way But Loose*), overheard passing conversations... You name it, I've taken it, knitted it together with something else and produced a book out of it.

For *Meant to Be Mine*, I took just the barest shell surrounding two of my daughter's friends (a married couple who happen to be wonderful teachers), said to myself "what if?" and used my imagination to fill in the blanks. What you have before you are the filled-in blanks. I hope you like it and are entertained.

As always, I thank you for taking the time to read one of my books. Without you, there would be nothing. And from the bottom of my heart, I wish you someone to love who loves you back.

Love,

Marie Ferrarella

Meant to be Mine

Marie Ferrarella

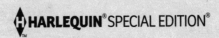

HARLEQUIN® SPECIAL EDITION®

Recycling programs
for this product may
not exist in your area.

ISBN-13: 978-0-373-62340-2

Meant to be Mine

Copyright © 2017 by Marie Rydzynski-Ferrarella

All rights reserved. Except for use in any review, the reproduction or utilization of this work in whole or in part in any form by any electronic, mechanical or other means, now known or hereinafter invented, including xerography, photocopying and recording, or in any information storage or retrieval system, is forbidden without the written permission of the publisher, Harlequin Enterprises Limited, 225 Duncan Mill Road, Don Mills, Ontario M3B 3K9, Canada.

This is a work of fiction. Names, characters, places and incidents are either the product of the author's imagination or are used fictitiously, and any resemblance to actual persons, living or dead, business establishments, events or locales is entirely coincidental.

This edition published by arrangement with Harlequin Books S.A.

For questions and comments about the quality of this book, please contact us at CustomerService@Harlequin.com.

® and TM are trademarks of Harlequin Enterprises Limited or its corporate affiliates. Trademarks indicated with ® are registered in the United States Patent and Trademark Office, the Canadian Intellectual Property Office and in other countries.

Printed in U.S.A.

www.Harlequin.com

A12006 903768

USA TODAY bestselling and RITA® Award–winning author **Marie Ferrarella** has written more than two hundred and fifty books for Harlequin, some under the name Marie Nicole. Her romances are beloved by fans worldwide. Visit her website, marieferrarella.com.

Visit the Author Profile page
at Harlequin.com for more titles.

To
Tiffany Khauo-Melgar
&
Edy Melgar

Wishing You Happiness
Forever
&
Always

And
To the Memory of Anne J. Nocton
My Fifth Grade Teacher
Who First Made Me Believe I Had Talent

Prologue

Tiffany Lee's eyes lit up the moment that she saw him.

She might only be four years old, but she was a woman who knew her own heart and her heart belonged to Monty. That was what he told her his name was when she got up the nerve to ask him.

Monty.

His family lived in the house down the block and had only been there a couple of months, but it was long enough for her to make up her mind that when she grew up, she was going to marry him.

"Let's go, Tiffany, you are making your sisters late for school," her mother scolded.

She was deliberately dawdling, hanging back until Monty could catch up to her. He went to her school, as did his sisters.

"I'm trying to button my sweater, Mama," she

said, seizing the first excuse she could think of. It was a cool spring morning and her sweater was hanging open because she'd put the buttons into the wrong holes and had to start again.

Her mother looked at her impatiently. She had rules about being late. Mama had rules about everything. She said you couldn't grow up properly without rules to guide you.

"You do not need to button your sweater, it is not cold," Mei-Li Lee told her youngest born. "Just hold it against you. Now come!"

"I can help you button that," the boy who had caught her young heart offered, coming up to her. "It won't take long," he promised.

She stood their, perfectly still, watching as his fingers pushed each button on her sweater through a hole. She felt like a princess and he was her prince.

And someday, she thought again, he would be her husband.

"Take your time, dear," Theresa Manetti told the dignified looking, slightly flustered Asian-American woman sitting in the chair beside her desk. "I have all afternoon."

That wasn't entirely true. At the moment Theresa had approximately half an hour to spare, but she didn't want the other woman to feel pressured or rushed.

They were sitting in her back office. The owner of a thriving catering company that had enjoyed more than a dozen years of success, Theresa had practically every minute of her time accounted for. But the award-winning chef trusted her people to capably carry on without her supervision for however long it took her friend, Mrs. Mei-Li Lee, to get around to asking what Theresa already knew in her heart the woman wanted to ask.

Having been involved in the side endeavor that she and her two lifelong best friends, Maizie Sommers and Cecilia Parnell, had been pursuing with passion and zest for a number of years, Theresa knew it was extremely difficult for some people to ask for help with such a delicate matter.

This was obviously the case for Mei-Li, whom she already knew was by nature a very private person.

Although Theresa was proud of her catering business, just as Maizie was proud of the real estate firm she had built from scratch and Cecilia was proud of her expanding house cleaning service, she felt that matchmaking was her true calling.

None of them took a penny for bringing about the matches they arranged, but it was no secret that they all felt richly rewarded by their successful ventures just the same. All three believed that there was something indescribably magical about bringing about these matches between soul mates who might have had no way of finding one another without a little outside "help."

"Maybe I'm being selfish," Mei-Li said, twisting the handkerchief she held in her hands until it began to look as if it was a little white corkscrew.

"You?" Theresa gently scoffed. "I know you, Mei-Li. You do not have a selfish bone in your entire body."

"But all of my other girls are married," the petite woman went on, referring to her four older daughters. "Two of them have children and Jennifer is expecting her first. Four out of five should be enough for any mother, shouldn't it?" she asked, raising her dark eyes to look at Theresa.

They might have different cultural backgrounds, but Theresa understood exactly where the other woman was coming from.

"You're not being selfish, Mei-Li. You're just being a mother. Mothers want to see *all* their children happily married. They want all of their children to have someone to love who loves them back. It's only natural, dear," Theresa assured her.

Mei-Li sighed, no doubt grateful for her friend's reassurance. "Tiffany would be so annoyed with me if she knew I was doing this," she confided.

Theresa reached across the desk, covering her friend's hand with her own. "Tiffany will never know," she promised with a knowing smile.

Mei-Li looked as if she was at a loss as to how her part in this undertaking could remain a secret. "But then how—"

"Trust me, the other ladies and I have been at this for a while now." Her warm smile widened. "Arrangements are made so that everything that 'happens' appears to be strictly by chance—and by luck," she added with an amused wink. "My own two children would have been horrified if they knew their mother had brought into their lives the individuals they ended up marrying.

"I'm sure you'll agree that if Tiffany doesn't know that you have any part in this, her natural inclination to resist won't get in the way and half the battle will be won right from the beginning."

Mei-Li sighed again. "I suppose you're right."

Theresa merely continued smiling, refraining from saying that of course she was right. When it came to matters of the heart, that was a given. All was fair in love and war—especially in love. Maizie had taught her that.

"Now, in order for us to get this little venture under way," Theresa said to the other woman, "I'm going to need more information from you about your lovely youngest daughter."

Mei-Li slowly relaxed. "Anything," she willingly agreed.

"Good," Theresa replied, pulling out an old-fashioned pad and pen to take notes. Some things, she felt, could not be improved on. "If everything goes well—and they always have up until now—my guess is that we should have Tiffany engaged, if not married, by Christmas."

There was no way to describe the look on Mei-Li's face other than pure, unadulterated joy.

As for Theresa, she couldn't wait to collect the information she needed to get this newest mission of the heart under way and to call her friends with the good news. Tonight she, Maizie and Cilia were going to be playing cards—and making arrangements to take the necessary steps that would bring love into Tiffany Lee's life.

Chapter One

"Do you have a minute, Ms. Sommers?"

Maizie Sommers had heard the door to her real estate office open a moment before she heard the deep, resonant voice politely addressing her. In the middle of writing up a glowing ad highlighting the features of a brand-new property she had just agreed to sell, Maizie held up her left hand, silently requesting another second. She wanted to jot down a thought before she responded.

Finished, Maizie looked up to see Eduardo Montoya, the handsome young handyman she had been recommending to any and all of her clients who needed a little work done on their residences. He was standing quietly by her desk, waiting for her to complete what she was doing.

She couldn't help thinking that he looked like every young woman's fantasy come to life.

"For you, Eddie, I have a whole hour." Putting down her pen, she smiled at him. She already knew what he had come to tell her, but for the sake of moving things along smoothly, she would pretend to be in the dark. "But you didn't need to stop by the office before going to see that lady about the bathroom remodel she wanted. I left all the details about it on your answering machine."

Eddie nodded, his straight, midnight-black hair moving ever so slightly around his face. "I got them and I appreciate the referral," he told her with cheerful sincerity. "I appreciate all the referrals you've been sending my way."

"I send them your way because you do excellent work," Maizie pointed out. Because she already knew what this visit was about, she smiled encouragingly at the young man. And because he couldn't know her part in arranging things to happen, she continued to look as if she was in the dark. "I sense a 'but' coming," she told him.

He flashed her a quick, easy smile, the kind that was capable of melting any young woman's heart. Seeing it made Maizie wonder, not for the first time, how in heaven's name Eddie still managed to remain unattached at twenty-eight.

There was a look in his eyes that spoke of excitement and happiness. Did it have anything to do with the new position he was starting on Monday morning? A position she not only knew about, but had a hand in facilitating, even if the young man had no idea of that.

Maizie waited patiently for Eddie to find the right words in order to tell her.

She didn't have long to wait. "That's why I wanted to come by and see you, so that I could tell you this in person."

Maizie continued to maintain her cheerful, warm expression, waiting for him to tell her his "news." She'd known Eddie Montoya for the last nine months, ever since one of her clients had recommended him when she needed some concrete work done on her own patio, and the contractor she'd usually used had retired and moved away. From the very beginning, Eddie's work ethic, not to mention the caliber of the work that he did, had left her exceedingly impressed.

So much so that she began to send business his way whenever any of her clients—be they recent home buyers or home sellers—needed work done. It quickly became apparent that Eddie's expertise went far beyond just cement work. It actually knew no bounds. The young man could lay brick, do landscaping as well as hardscaping, and was able to build room additions with the best of them.

Eddie's late father, she'd learned, had been in the construction business and had actually built the house that Eddie and his two older sisters had grown up in. His mother, he told her, still lived there.

"Take a seat," Maizie invited, gesturing to the chair beside her desk. Once he had lowered his five-foot-ten muscular frame into it, she hospitably asked, "Can I get you something to drink?" She gestured to the well-stocked counter against the back wall behind her. "Coffee? Tea? Bottled water?"

"No, ma'am, I'm fine, thank you," Eddie told her politely.

Maizie folded her hands and inclined her head.

"All right, then let's get to this 'but' that's hovering between us. What is it that you came to tell me that you couldn't tell me over the phone?"

He cleared his throat, then began. "Well, Ms. Sommers, you've been so nice to me, I didn't want you thinking I was leaving you high and dry."

"*Are* you leaving me high and dry?" Maizie asked, wondering if this was going to turn out to be about something else, after all.

She hoped not. She and her friends Theresa and Cilia had brainstormed for the last two days, starting the same evening that Theresa had been approached by her friend regarding the woman's remaining unattached daughter. The moment Theresa had shown them the photograph of Tiffany Lee, which the young woman's mother had given her, something inside Maizie's head had "clicked" as everything had just fallen into place.

Although the names of a couple of other potential candidates had been brought up, Maizie's mind insisted on returning to Eddie. With very little effort, she could actually *see* the two together—and the babies they would have.

From that moment on, she'd been completely sold on the idea that Eddie was the right match for Tiffany, and she had in short order sold both her friends on the idea, as well.

And now he was sitting here in her office, at her desk, looking suddenly very solemn. Was he possibly about to send her hopes for another perfect match tumbling into an abyss?

Mentally crossing her fingers, Maizie waited for him to speak.

"No. Well, not exactly," he answered, correcting himself.

"Then what, 'exactly,' dear?" Maizie asked, gently coaxing the words out of him.

"Well, you know that I'm not really a contractor by trade," Eddie began, referring to what he had told her when he had first come to work for the woman.

"Yes, I know, but you do an extremely good imitation of one," she told him, smiling.

As with everyone she came in contact with, Maizie knew the young man's backstory. Eduardo Montoya was an elementary schoolteacher. A very gifted one, if the way she'd seen him interacting with children was any indication of his abilities. Due to recent drastic cutbacks in the district where he had been employed, he had lost his job and was forced to pick up work as a substitute teacher, which was the only thing that had been available to him at the time.

However, because those jobs were few and far between, Eddie had needed some way to fill in the gaps. He did it by picking up odd jobs that other contractors turned down.

Although he was single, with no mortgage payments to worry about, only rent, he did have school loans he needed to repay. Unlike some young people Maizie was acquainted with, Eddie refused to let his loans mount up without making any payments. On the contrary, he was determined to repay the entire amount as quickly as he could. Because of that sense of honor, he picked up anything that Maizie and her friends sent his way, and sometimes wound up working seven days a week.

He started slowly. "Before I came to work for you, I was a teacher,"

"*Are*," Maizie corrected, cutting in. "You *are* a teacher, Eddie."

He flashed her another warm smile, obviously pleased that she thought of him in that light. "And now a position's come up."

"Teaching?" Maizie asked, hoping she didn't sound too innocent as she put the question to him.

The fact was, she knew all about this. Knew because she was actually the one behind his being hired for the position. Not in the initial part, which involved a young teacher going into premature labor, but in the ultimate outcome. Because of her connections, Maizie had been able to get his résumé moved to the front of the line.

For now, she did her best to look intrigued and interested—and very hopeful for the young man she had come to regard so highly during their brief association.

"Yes, teaching," Eddie answered. "It seems that one of the teachers at Bedford's newest school, that elementary school that was just opened last fall, Bedford Elementary, went into early labor yesterday— *really* early," he emphasized. "From what I heard, she wasn't due for another month."

"She went into labor four weeks early?" Maizie questioned, genuinely concerned. Her connection hadn't mentioned this part to her—undoubtedly because they knew she would be concerned. "I hope the baby's all right."

Eddie nodded, pleased to be the bearer of good

news not just for himself, but all around. "I asked," he told her. "Mother and baby are both doing fine."

Hearing this, Maizie blinked, admittedly somewhat surprised.

"You know the mother?" she inquired. This was another piece of information she hadn't gotten previously. It really was a small world.

"What? Oh, no, I don't," Eddie said, quickly setting the record straight. "I just asked the administrator about the teacher when they called me about the sudden vacancy."

Maizie looked at him, once again very pleased with her choice for Mei-Li's daughter. "You're an unusual young man, Eddie. Most men your age wouldn't have inquired about the mother's condition." *Or asked any other questions of a personal nature that didn't directly include them,* she added silently.

"I grew up with two older sisters and a mother. If I hadn't thought to ask, they would have skinned me," he told her simply, taking no credit for the fact that he really was a thoughtful, sensitive young man.

As it happened, Maizie had sold the principal of this new elementary school her house when Ada Walters had first moved to the area, and as was her habit, Maizie had remained on friendly terms with her client long after the ink had dried on the mortgage papers.

Once Theresa had supplied her the information about their newest client-in-search-of-a-match, she had called the principal to find out if Ada knew of any upcoming openings in either her school or any of others nearby. As luck would have it, there was one in the offing in the near future.

And then the future became the immediate present.

When she'd heard about the sudden opening, Maizie had immediately brought up Eddie's name and his qualifications. And just like that, the pieces fell into place, as her instincts had told her they would.

But Maizie never left anything to chance and never allowed herself to grow too confident, no matter how foolproof a situation might look. So when Eddie had walked into her office just now, looking a tad uncomfortable, Maizie had braced herself—just in case—and then was relieved to discover that it had been a false alarm.

So far, it was all going according to plan, and she couldn't be more pleased.

"You've come to tell me that you're going to have to turn down that last job I sent your way," she guessed. That wasn't a disaster; it just put off the inevitable. The two were still going to meet at the school, where Tiffany taught fifth grade, now that Eddie was taking over Chelsea Jamison's third-grade class.

"Oh no, I'm still going to do that." He was quick to set her straight. "It's just that I'm going to have to get started on the remodel early tomorrow morning, and do my best to finish up by late Sunday night."

"And if you can't?" Maizie asked, always wanting to remain one step ahead of any surprises.

"Then I'll have to come back next weekend so I can get the job done," he told her. "Do you think that'll be a problem?"

The young man was one in a million, Maizie couldn't help thinking.

"The kind of work you do, Eddie," she told him,

"I'm sure that the home owner will be more than happy to accommodate you."

He glanced at his watch, a gift from his mother when he had graduated from college. He never took it off. Pressed for time, he realized he had to be getting back.

"I'm just finishing up this other job, so I won't be able to give the home owner a proper estimate until I get there tomorrow morning and look the job over." He didn't believe in quoting one price and then upping it as the work got under way. He took pride in keeping his costs, and thus his prices, low.

"That's no problem at all," Maizie assured him. "The owner's mother is paying for it. She referred to it as an early birthday present. She told me to tell you that as long as you don't wind up charging anything exorbitant, she'll be all right with your fee." Maizie smiled at the young man, delighted with the way this was going. "I told her you were very reasonable. She was happy you were taking the job."

Eddie laughed. "I guess that means I'll just have to put that Hawaiian vacation I was planning on hold," he quipped.

"Of course you will," Maizie deadpanned. "Don't forget, you have children to educate now." Unable to maintain a serious expression any longer, she allowed herself to smile, radiating genuine warmth. The kind of warmth that had clients, and people in general, trusting her instantly. "I'm very happy for you, Eddie. I know that you feel that teaching is your calling. I really hate to lose you, but if I have to, I'm glad it's for this reason."

"Well, you're not exactly 'losing' me, Ms. Sommers," Eddie told her almost shyly, exposing a side to her that most people didn't see. "I still do have those student loans to pay back so I'll need to pick up those extra jobs on weekends—as long as your clients won't mind having me around then, working. I'll do my best not to get underfoot," he promised earnestly.

Maizie laughed. It was obvious that the young man before her didn't realize just how rare a competent worker was. "Eddie, considering the prices you charge and the work you do, I'm fairly certain they would be willing to put up with all sorts of crazy hours on your part."

She sat back, thoughtfully regarding him for a moment. "So, just to be sure, I can tell Ms. Lee that you'll be at her house tomorrow morning?"

His grin lit up the office. Maizie saw that her assistant looked utterly entranced as she glanced in their direction. "Absolutely," Eddie said.

Maizie clapped her hands together and declared, "Wonderful!"

Eddie looked at the address on the piece of paper again. Specifically, at the name that appeared right over the address and beneath the phone number he'd been given in case he needed to cancel the appointment or to change the time he'd be arriving.

With everything that had been happening these last couple days, the name, when he'd heard it, hadn't fully registered. It did now.

Tiffany Lee.

Could it actually be her?

No, Eddie told himself, he was letting his imagination get carried away. Neither Tiffany nor Lee was an uncommon name, and he was fairly certain that even if he Googled them together, or searched through Facebook, he would find more than a handful of "Tiffany Lees." And none would be the Tiffany Lee he remembered from college who was, hands down, the most argumentative woman on the face of the earth.

Or more importantly, the same Tiffany Lee he had had a crush on—when she was four and he was five—before she had become such a competitive pain.

Damn silly thing to remember now, Eddie thought, pulling his car up in front of the modest looking two-story house. What his mind *should* be on now was doing a good job for this woman, getting paid and focusing any spare time he might have tonight and tomorrow night on getting fully prepared to take over Chelsea Jamison's third-grade class.

He'd already done his due diligence as far as that was concerned. The moment he'd learned from the principal that he would be taking over the woman's class, he'd requested a list of the students' names and any sort of notes Chelsea might have made regarding the individual students.

Eddie prided himself on never going in cold or unprepared. This way, there would be no awkward period of adjustment. He wanted the students to respond to him immediately. To feel as if he was their mentor, or at least someone who was willing to listen to what they had to say—both in the class and privately, if they needed help with something of a more personal nature, like being bullied.

He loved teaching, and wanted to leave a memorable impression on the students he encountered. More than that, he wanted to, by his own example, encourage the kids he'd be dealing with to make the most of their potential. Had his fifth-grade teacher, Miss Nocton, not done that for him, not seen past his cocky bravado, he might be languishing in a prison somewhere right now, like some of the guys from his old neighborhood. But Miss Nocton, a dour-faced, straitlaced woman, had awakened a thirst for knowledge within him by challenging him. Every time he felt that he had done his best, she had told him he could do better.

And damned if he couldn't, Eddie thought now with a smile. Granted, he had a great family and he loved his mother and his sisters, but it was that little, no-nonsense woman in the sensible shoes who was responsible for the fact that he was who he was today. He intended to make her proud, even if she was no longer around to see it.

Eddie took a deep breath. *Time to get to work,* he told himself.

Shelving his thoughts, he reached over and rang the doorbell.

Chapter Two

Tiffany Lee was not fully awake as she stumbled down the stairs and toward the annoying noise. Her eyes were still in the process of trying to focus. It was the sound of the doorbell that had disrupted her sleep and eventually forced her out of bed to answer it—because it just wouldn't stop ringing.

She had never been accused of being a morning person. She was especially not a *weekend* morning person. Five days a week, she resigned herself to the fact that she had to be up and smiling at an ungodly hour—and any hour before 9:00 a.m. was ungodly in her book. But her job called for her to be up and at 'em early.

Someday, when she became queen of the world, school wouldn't begin until noon, she promised herself. But until that glorious day arrived, Tiffany knew she had to make every effort to turn up in her classroom before eight in the morning. That way, when her students marched in shortly after eight, everything would be ready and waiting for them—including her. Because she really loved teaching and loved her students, she went along with this soul-crushing arrangement.

But weekends were supposed to be her own. And in a perfect world, they would be. But in a perfect world, bathroom sinks and bathtub faucets didn't suddenly give up the ghost and gurgle instead of producing water—and toilets would flush with breathtaking regularity rather than just 50 percent of the time. None of that was presently happening in the master bath adjacent to her bedroom, and she knew she needed help—desperately. It was either that or start sleeping downstairs near the other bathroom, something she had begun to seriously consider.

Her mother, for once, hadn't somehow turned her current dilemma into yet another excuse to go on and on about how this just showed why Tiffany needed a husband in her life. A husband who would take care of all these annoying nuisances whenever they cropped up.

Instead of bending her ear, her mother, bless her, had not only volunteered to find someone to put an end to her master bathroom woes, she had even said she would pay for it.

The only catch was that the contractor had to come do the work on the weekend because he had a day job the rest of the week.

She hadn't realized when she'd agreed to her mother's generous offer that "weekend" meant the very start of the weekend—and that it apparently started before daylight made its appearance.

So okay, Tiffany thought, dragging her hand through her hair—as if that motion would somehow cause adrenaline to go shooting through the rest of her very sleepy body—technically "weekend" meant any time after midnight, Friday, but she'd figured she would have some leeway.

Obviously not, she thought with a deep sigh.

The ringing sounded even more shrill as she got closer. It felt as if it was jarring everything within her that was jarrable.

"I'm coming, I'm coming," she cried irritably, raising her voice so it could be heard through the door. "Hold your horses. The bathroom's not going anywhere."

Glancing through the peephole, she made out what looked to be some sort of a truck parked at her curb. There was someone in dark blue coveralls standing on her front step.

The contractor her mother sent—she hoped.

The plot thickens, Tiffany whimsically thought. feeling slightly giddy.

"Good to know," Eddie said the moment she unlocked the door and pulled it partially open.

Her brain still foggy, Tiffany blinked at him. "Excuse me?"

He grinned at her. She caught herself thinking that it was way too early for a smile that cheerful. Was there something wrong with the man her mother had sent?

There was something oddly familiar about that smile—but the thought was gone before she could catch it and she was way too tired to make the effort to try to place it.

"You said that the bathroom wasn't going anywhere and I responded, 'Good to know,' since I'm going to be working on remodeling it," Eddie told her, patiently explaining his comment. Teaching younger students had taught him to have infinite patience.

"Oh." She supposed that made sense.

Functioning on a five-second delay, Tiffany opened the door wider, allowing the good-looking contractor to come inside. The rather large toolbox in his hand convinced her that he was on the level. Who carried around something that big at this hour of the morning if they didn't have to?

"Sorry," she apologized. "My brain doesn't usually kick in this early in the morning."

"Early?" he echoed in amusement. "You think this is early?"

"I don't think," she said, followed by a yawn she couldn't stifle. "I know." She started for the stairs. Glancing over her shoulder, she saw that the man with the toolbox wasn't following her. "The bathroom's upstairs." She pointed for emphasis.

"Wait," he called out, bringing her to a halt. The woman was either way too trusting or simply naive—and he had to admit that she didn't look to be either. Especially if she turned out to be who he thought she was. "Don't you want to see my credentials?"

Tiffany yawned again, not at his question, but because her body desperately yearned to go back to bed and she couldn't.

"You're driving what looks like a service truck, you've got on coveralls and you're carrying around the biggest toolbox I've ever seen. Those are credentials enough for me."

Besides, she added mentally, *knowing my mother, you probably already got the third degree before she hired you.*

"What about my estimate?" he asked. They hadn't talked about what he was going to charge her for the work. He didn't plan to overcharge her, but she didn't know that. "I haven't given you one because I need to see the bathroom first."

Tiffany waved away his words. "I don't need to hear it," she told him as she began to walk up the stairs. "My mother insisted on paying for this remodel, and after arguing with that woman about everything else under the sun ever since I could talk, I thought that this one time I'd just give in and say yes.

"Your bill," she told him as he followed behind her, "will go to her, and trust me, if you try to fleece her, you will live to regret it—immensely. My mother's a little woman, but she's definitely a force to be reckoned with. None of my brothers-in-law will go up against her. They've learned that if they want to keep living, they need to stay on her good side," she concluded as they reached the bathroom he was going to be remodeling.

The door was standing open and she gestured toward the interior. "Here it is," she said needlessly. "Knock yourself out."

And with that, she turned on her bare heel and walked away.

This had to be the most unorthodox job he'd ever been called to. "Wait, don't you want to tell me what you want?" Eddie asked, calling after her retreating back.

Tiffany only half turned in his direction. She wanted nothing more than to get dressed and then collapse on the bed in the guest room for a few hours. She assumed that the man her mother had sent didn't need any supervision. He appeared competent enough.

"I want a bathroom," she told him. "One where everything works, 24/7. And it would be nice if everything matched."

"Well, of course it's going to work," he told her. That's why he was here, and he wasn't about to do a shoddy job. But her answer didn't begin to address his question. "What about the style? And the color?" he pressed.

There was something familiar about his voice, but like his smile, she couldn't place it and she wasn't up to thinking right now. Her brain was foggy. Maybe it was just her imagination.

"Style and color would be good," she replied, nodding as she began to walk away again.

Eddie took a breath. He realized that the woman with the gorgeous legs and the football jersey wasn't being flippant. She apparently still wasn't fully awake.

She shouldn't have answered the door half-asleep. He couldn't help thinking that she really was in need of a keeper.

Eddie tilted his head a little, trying to get a better look at her face. Her shiny, long, blue-black hair kept falling into it. His curiosity was becoming more aroused, but he really didn't need to have it satisfied in order to do a good job.

It would just be nice to know what his client actually looked like.

And then she turned slightly in his direction and it hit him like a ton of bricks. It was her, the Tiffany he knew in college. The Tiffany who was so different from the little girl whose sweater he'd buttoned all those years ago.

He wanted to tell her, then thought better of it. Now wasn't the time. He'd tell her after the job was done.

Pushing back that thought, he tried to pin her down again—at least a little bit. "What do you like? Modern? Antique? Classic?"

The words he tossed her way seemed to circle around her head, even though she tried to visualize the styles. Tiffany had a feeling he wouldn't give her any peace until she made some kind of a choice.

So she did.

"Modern," she told him.

Heading back toward the stairs, she heard him declare, "Well, that's a start."

Feeling she needed to acknowledge his response, she nodded. "Yes, it is." Then, just to keep things civilized, she added, "If you want coffee, help yourself. There's a coffee machine in the kitchen. It's on a timer."

Having reached the banister, she ran her hand along the sleek light wood as she made her way down the stairs. When she reached the bottom, she quickly hurried to the back bedroom, flipped the lock on the door—just in case—and arrived at her real destination: the guest room bed.

A sigh of relief escaped her lips as she collapsed on the mattress.

The last thought that floated through her mind was that there was something vaguely familiar about the man who had come to remodel her bathroom.

The next moment, it was gone.

Tiffany felt like she had been lying down for only a few minutes when the noise suddenly started.

It was loud enough to have her bolting upright, abruptly terminating what was beginning to be a pleasant semisleep.

Glancing at the clock on the nightstand, she saw that she'd actually been asleep for half an hour, but that was far from enough. Especially since the noise turned out to be steady enough to keep her from putting her head back on the pillow. And it was definitely irritating enough to keep her from falling asleep again.

"He's actually working," she muttered incredulously. "Who does that as soon as they arrive?"

The noise gave no sign of abating. For the second time that day Tiffany got out of bed. But this time, rather than heading for the door and the annoying doorbell, she went in search of the source of the teeth-jarring noise.

Hanging on to the banister, she half walked, half dragged herself up the stairs, all the while struggling to finally wake up—permanently. There was no point in even *thinking* that she could go back to sleep again. That ship had definitely sailed.

Once on the landing, Tiffany made her way toward the source of the noise, which was growing louder with every step she took. It was emanating from just beyond her bedroom, she discovered. Specifically, from her master bathroom.

The noise seemed to vibrate right through her chest.

Standing in the doorway, Tiffany looked accusingly at the culprit behind her shattered morning's sleep. "Why are you destroying my bathroom?" she asked.

Covered in dust and wearing a mask over his face to keep from breathing it in, Eddie looked for a moment at the woman whose bathroom he was remodeling, before setting down the sledgehammer he'd been wielding. He pushed the mask to the top of his head and answered her question.

"Well, for one thing, I can't put the new fixtures in without getting the old ones out," he told her. He gestured around the bathroom. "That includes your bathroom tub, sink, medicine cabinet and commode."

Commode? That certainly was a delicate way to talk about the toilet, she thought, somewhat surprised.

Tiffany blinked, and for the first time since she had let the man into her house, she actually *looked* at him. Not through him, around him or over him, but *at* him. And now that she did, even though her brain was still just a wee bit foggy and out of sync, she realized that there really was something vaguely familiar about the man standing in her bathroom, effectively making rubble out of it.

Where did she know him from? Nothing specific came to mind, though a memory seemed to play hide-and-seek with her brain, vanishing before she could get hold of it.

The next moment, she let it go, focusing on the more important question for the time being. "You do know what you're doing, don't you?"

Amusement curved the corners of his mouth as Eddie watched her for an incredibly long minute. "It's a little late to be asking that, isn't it?" He looked around at the rubble he'd created. "You didn't ask to see any letters of reference, or photographs of my previous work."

"I assumed my mother had you vetted," she replied. "Which is good enough for me. She's like a little barracuda. Nothing gets past her."

He understood what she was telling him, but it hadn't been like that. The woman who'd called him, saying she'd gotten his number from Ms. Sommers, had just said that her daughter's bathroom needed remodeling and to use his better judgment. He'd found that rather unusual. He found Tiffany being so lax about it even more unusual.

Maybe she had become less intense over the years. After all, it had been five years since he'd last seen her. The Tiffany he remembered from their classes together in college had been extremely competitive and had had to verify everything for herself. She'd also given him one hell of a run for his money. Maybe it was a good thing that she didn't recognize him just yet. He did need the money this job would yield. For now, he decided to play this by ear.

"I just thought you'd want to ask some questions yourself," he told her.

"Okay," she said. "How long is this going to take?" When he made no attempt to answer, Tiffany gestured at her disintegrated bathroom. "This," she emphasized, moving her hand to encompass the entire spacious room. "All this. Rebuilding it. How long is this going to take?" she repeated, enunciating every word.

Leaning the sledgehammer against a wall, Eddie dusted himself off. "'This' is turning out to be a bigger job than I thought it was going to be."

She gave her own interpretation to his words. "Is that your clever way of asking for more money? Because I already told you that my mother—"

"No," Eddie said, cutting her off before she could get wound up. The Tiffany he remembered could get *really* wound up. "I'm asking for more *time*. I thought your bathroom could be remodeled in a weekend, but now that I see it, I realize it's going to take at least two."

She still didn't understand why this contractor could work on the bathroom only on weekends. It didn't make any sense to her. "Why not just come back Monday morning and keep at it until it's finished?" she demanded.

Eddie inclined his head, as if conceding the point—sort of. "A week ago, I would have agreed—"

"Fine," she declared, satisfied that she'd won this argument. "Then it's settled—"

Eddie talked right over her. As he recalled from past encounters with Tiffany, it was the only way to get his point across. "But that was before I took a day job."

She assumed he was talking about another construction job. "Put it off until you're finished."

He shook his head. "I'm afraid that's not possible."

"*Anything* is possible," Tiffany insisted. "I know that you construction people take on multiple jobs."

Her best friend had dated a man who had his own construction company, and she'd complained about taking second place to his work schedule. "That way, if one falls through, there's still enough work to keep you going."

"This isn't another construction job," Eddie informed her. "It's a different job entirely, in a different field."

He resisted the urge to explain just what that other job was. He wasn't superstitious by nature, but in this instance he was afraid that if he talked too much about the job that was waiting for him come Monday morning, somehow or other he'd wind up jinxing it. He loved working with his hands, loved creating something out of nothing, but construction work didn't begin to hold a candle to being a teacher. The one allowed him to create functional things; the other was instrumental in awakening sleeping minds, brains that were thirsting for knowledge. And amid those budding minds one could very well belong to someone who might do great things not just for one or two people, but for a multitude.

But Tiffany wasn't about to let this drop. He began to think that she hadn't changed, after all. "What kind of field?"

"A field that might eventually produce someone who could do something to effect the masses," he told her, leaving it at that.

"The masses?" she questioned, eyeing him as if he'd taken leave of his senses. "You make it sound as if you were part of the CIA."

"No, not that organization," he replied.

"But you won't talk about it?" she asked, really curious now.

"I'm not being paid to talk, I'm being paid to work," he reminded her, picking up the sledgehammer again. But Tiffany made no move to leave the area. She was obviously waiting for him to tell her what he was referring to. "I'd rather not jinx it," he finally told her, being quite honest.

She cocked her head, trying to reconcile a few things in her brain that just weren't meshing. "You're superstitious?"

"Just in this one respect."

"Good," she said, turning to leave as he began to work again. "Because superstitions are stupid."

It *was* her. If he'd had the slightest doubt before, he didn't anymore, Eddie decided. She was just as opinionated now as she had been then.

As she left the room, he slanted a long look in her direction. From there he couldn't see her face, only the back of her head. But even the set of her shoulders looked familiar.

It was Tiffany Lee, all right. And right now, he couldn't decide if that was a good thing or not. The only thing he knew was that he wasn't going say anything to her about their shared past. At least, not yet.

Chapter Three

Since Tiffany apparently didn't recognize him, Eddie decided to keep the fact that they had a history to himself and not say anything to her until he felt the time was right—like after he finished the job. After all, he couldn't have made that much of an impression on her if she didn't remember him. He vividly remembered their interactions in college, but it was obvious that she didn't. If he reminded her of it, she might just turn around and fire him.

It was best to leave well enough alone.

Working at a steady pace, he demolished the bathroom and then carted the debris out to his truck until it was filled, at which time he hauled it to the county dump. That involved a number of round trips. All in all, it took him practically the entire day.

He worked continuously, taking only one thirty-minute break to consume a fast-food lunch that was far from satisfying.

By four thirty, he was completely wiped out and decided to call it a day. But he didn't want to just pack up and leave, the way he knew some people in his line of work would. He wanted Tiffany to be made aware that he was leaving for the day. Otherwise, she might wind up thinking she had to wait around for him to return.

When he didn't see her during his multiple trips back and forth to his truck while he was packing up his tools and equipment, Eddie resigned himself to the fact that he was going to have to go looking for her. Since she hadn't said anything about leaving the house, he assumed she had to be on the premises *somewhere*.

As unobtrusively as possible, he went through both floors of the house, going from room to room.

Tiffany wasn't anywhere to be found.

Would she just leave the house—and him—without saying anything? Granted, it wasn't as if she had to check in with him, since technically, he was the one working for her. But just walking out without letting him know that she was going or when she'd be back didn't seem quite right to him.

What if something came up and he wanted to go home while she was out? He couldn't very well just leave her house standing wide open. That was tantamount to issuing an invitation to any burglar in the area. And despite the fact that if anything happened, it wouldn't be his fault, he would still feel responsible if someone *did* break in and steal something.

With a sigh, Eddie resigned himself to waiting for

her to come home. That was when he happened to glance out the rear bedroom window. It was facing the tidily trimmed backyard, which was where Tiffany had disappeared to.

She appeared to be completely engrossed in a book. She was sitting at a small oval table in the little gazebo that was off to one side of the yard.

He should have thought of looking there first! Eddie upbraided himself as he left the bedroom and hurried down the staircase. After all, it was a beautiful April day.

Since she had obviously taken it upon herself to stick around while he worked, he could understand Tiffany wanting to take advantage of the weather. Which explained why she was outside, reading a book.

After reaching the bottom of the stairs, Eddie went to the rear of the house and opened the sliding glass door. It groaned a little as he did so. He debated leaving the door open—after all, informing her that he was leaving for the day wasn't going to take any time, he reasoned. But then he thought better of it—just in case—and pulled the door closed again.

Despite the groaning noise, Tiffany didn't even look up.

She was totally engrossed in the book she was reading—a real book, he noted with a smile, not one of those electronic devices that held the entire contents of the Los Angeles Public Library within its slender, rectangular frame.

For a moment he said nothing. He almost hated to disturb her, but he really needed to get going.

His body ached from swinging his sledgehammer

and hauling out the wreckage that had been her bathroom just eight hours ago. What he craved right now
was a long, bracing shower with wave after wave of
hot, pulsating water hitting every tight muscle and
ache he had—and a few that he probably didn't even
know he had.

Eddie cleared his throat, waiting for her to look
up. But either she was too caught up in the story or
he was being too quiet, because Tiffany went right
on reading.

He tried clearing his throat again, much louder
this time. When that had no effect, he decided to say
something outright and tell her that he was leaving
for the day.

He had no idea exactly how to address her; calling
her "Ms. Lee" just didn't seem right to him, since the
very first time their paths had crossed they'd lived in
the same neighborhood. She'd been four and he'd been
five at the time. But given the nature of their present
relationship, he couldn't very well call her "Tiffany,"
at least not until she recognized him.

So after giving the matter as much thought as he
felt it deserved—which was very little—Eddie decided to forgo any salutation whatsoever and merely
announced in a resonant voice that was bound to get
her attention, "I'm leaving now."

Startled—Tiffany really *had* been engrossed in
the book she was reading, a fast-paced mystery by
one of her favorite writers—she looked up and was
truly surprised to find she was no longer alone in
the backyard.

Doing what she could to reestablish her poise, she

put down her book and then inquired almost regally, "You're finished?"

Eddie nodded. "For the day."

"But you're coming back tomorrow, right?" she asked a little uncertainly as she got up from the small redwood table.

"I said I'd finish remodeling the bathroom, so yes, I'm coming back." Since they were talking, he had a more important question for her. "Have you given any more thought to what you want?" Realizing she might find the sentence rather ambiguous, he quickly added, "In the way of colors? Fixtures? Styles?"

"I thought we agreed to leave that up to you." The truth was she hadn't given any thought to it at all.

He frowned slightly. "I didn't think you were serious."

There wasn't a woman alive who wouldn't want some sort of input when it came to decorating her living space. At least he'd never met one, he amended. Given how opinionated and stubborn he remembered Tiffany being, he sincerely doubted that he'd met one now.

"I'll make it easy for you," he told her. "There's an entire area in Anaheim that has store after store dealing with bathroom fixtures, tubs, medicine cabinets, tile and marble—"

But she shook her head, holding up her hand to stop him from going on. "There's no point in telling me where those stores are. I wouldn't know where to begin, or how much I needed of any particular thing," she told him.

Eddie frowned inwardly. He didn't want to put himself out there and volunteer to take her to the various shops. If nothing else, traipsing from one store to another would be very time consuming.

On the other hand, if he didn't offer to go with her, he'd have nothing to work on tomorrow or next weekend, and this project could drag on indefinitely. He needed the money sooner rather than later.

Besides, he wanted to be able to get his head together for the new class he'd be taking over Monday morning. It wasn't that he couldn't multitask, but he definitely preferred not having his mind going in two different directions at the same time. It was a lot less stressful that way.

And just like that, without a single shot being fired, Eddie surrendered.

"All right, why don't I take you to the different stores tomorrow?" he suggested. "That way, I can at least point you in the right direction and you can make the choices."

He waited for her to agree. Instead, Tiffany had a strange look on her face. Not as if she was thinking over his offer, but more like she was trying hard to place something.

It turned out to be him.

Out of the blue, her light blue eyes pinning him down, Tiffany suddenly asked, "Do I know you from somewhere?"

She'd almost succeeded in knocking him for a loop, but Eddie managed to regain control over himself and the situation. "Yes, I'm the guy who was swinging the sledgehammer in your master bathroom all day."

"No," Tiffany said impatiently, "I mean, do I know you from somewhere else?"

"Possibly," he allowed. "I've been lots of places." And then, because he didn't want to risk losing this job—he really did need every penny he could earn— he told her, "I've got to get going. I'm meeting some- one in an hour."

For just a split second, she felt her stomach drop. "Oh." Tiffany immediately took his response to mean that he had a date. She didn't want to seem to be trying to keep him here, especially if he did have a date—and why shouldn't he, considering his looks?

She was just trying to place him. It was probably her imagination, anyway, she decided. A lot of people looked like someone else at first scrutiny.

She took a breath, ready to wave him on. "Well, then I won't keep you."

Eddie gazed at her without commenting.

He'd told her a lie. He wasn't meeting anyone, but it was the first thing he could think of, and it must have done the trick because she was backing off.

Maybe he'd enlighten her tomorrow about why she thought she knew him. But he wasn't up to going into any of that tonight. Especially if, after he told her that they'd gone to school together and wound up competing against one another more than once, she decided to tell him to get lost. He needed to be fresh and on his toes if it turned out that he had to talk her out of terminating him.

So for now, Eddie quietly took his leave. "I'll be here early tomorrow," he told her, just before he turned toward the sliding-glass door.

"Of course you will," she murmured under her breath. She meant to say that to herself, but it was loud enough for him to hear.

He took it as a complaint about the time.

"All right, then how about eight thirty?" he proposed gamely, thinking that was a compromise.

It might have been, but obviously not in her eyes. "Eight thirty is still early," she pointed out.

He wondered if she was being deliberately difficult or if it was just an unconscious reaction on her part. "It's half an hour later than this morning."

"Half an hour only means something if you're a fruit fly," she said in exasperation. "What time do those stores you mentioned open?"

He didn't have to think to answer. All this had become second nature to him in the last few months, ever since he'd lost his teaching position. "They open up at eleven on Sunday."

It wasn't perfect, but it was better, she thought, and she said as much out loud. "Okay, come at ten thirty," she instructed.

He didn't like getting a late start, not when there were other things he could do while he was waiting to take her on that hardware safari.

"If I come earlier, I can do prep work," he told her. That was important, since he was fairly confident they were bound to come home with at least some of the things needed to remodel her bathroom.

"If you come later," she countered, "then I can sleep."

"You can *always* sleep," he responded. "Besides, sleep is highly overrated."

Tiffany could feel her blood pressure rising. This was the most annoyingly stubborn man… Regrouping, she blew out a breath.

"Tell you what, let's compromise. You can come

here at eight." She shuddered as she contemplated the early hour. "As long as you promise not to make any noise. And I get to sleep until it's time to leave for those store you're so anxious to have me go to."

Eddie suppressed a frown. He knew it was useless to argue; and if memory served him correctly, Tiffany could argue the ears off of a brass monkey without blinking an eye.

So he gave in. "You're the boss," he finally told her.

In response to his capitulation, her grin was positively beatific.

"Yes, I am, aren't I?" Anxious to have him leave before he changed his mind, she quickly led the way to the front door. "Okay, see you tomorrow." Tiffany opened it and held it wide. "Have a good night," she said as she waved him on his way.

She thought she heard him grunt in response, but she wasn't sure.

What she did know was that the house was suddenly quiet.

Blissfully, wonderfully quiet.

After a few moments, though, it seemed almost *too* quiet. Especially after all the noise she had endured for most of the day.

"I've got to be going crazy," she muttered.

Turning away, she headed into the living room. She was just about to turn on the TV—which was her usual method of combating the almost oppressive late-afternoon quiet—when she heard the doorbell ring.

Now what?

With a sigh, Tiffany pivoted on her heel and hurried back to the front door. Without stopping to look through the peephole to make sure it was the contractor, she opened the door and asked, "Did you forget something?"

"Not that I know of. But perhaps you have forgotten your manners."

It wasn't the contractor. Instead, there on her front step was five-feet-nothing of angst and the source of not a few of her headaches.

Too surprised to even force a smile, Tiffany asked, "Mother, what are you doing here?"

The model-slender woman raised her small chin. "Is that any way to greet the woman who gave you life?"

That was her mother's opening salvo in almost every exchange they had. "It is if I'm not expecting to see the woman who gave me life."

Mei-Li shook her head. "Someday, when I am gone, you will wish that you could see me just one more time," she told her youngest daughter, uttering the words like a prophecy. "But for now, while I am still alive, you should *always* expect to see me."

Rather than ask if that was supposed to be some sort of a curse, Tiffany took a breath. She stepped back and opened her door a little wider—her mother didn't need much room to come in.

Trying again, Tiffany asked in her best upbeat tone, "And to what do I owe this unexpected pleasure, dear Mother?"

Mei-Li did not appear placated. "There is no need to be sarcastic, Tiffany."

Tiffany squelched the temptation to raise her voice in total frustration. Instead, she struggled for patience and tried a third time, keeping her voice even and respectful, despite the fact that to her own ear, it sounded almost singsong. "Mother, is there something I can do for you?"

Walking in, the small woman scanned the room, taking in everything at once even as she rolled her eyes in response to the question. "More things than I could possibly enumerate in the space of a day," she replied.

"But you didn't come to enumerate a long list of things," Tiffany pointed out. "I know you, Mother. You came here for a very specific reason. You always do," she added as her mom opened her mouth to deny the assumption. "Now what is it?"

"How was he?" her mother asked without any preamble.

Tiffany was caught completely off guard, her mind a total blank. "'He?'"

Mei-Li sighed, exasperated. "Surely you are not so dumb as you pretend, Tiffany. The young man I am paying to remodel your bathroom," she said with emphasis. "Did he do a good job?"

She made it sound as if renovating a bathroom could be done in a single afternoon. *If only,* Tiffany thought wistfully. But at the same time, the question irritated her. "Mother, he's just gotten started."

To her surprise, her mother actually seemed pleased rather than annoyed that the job hadn't been magically completed.

"Oh. Good," Mei-Li commented. Then, because they were supposed to be discussing remodeling the bathroom and not remodeling her stubborn daughter's life, she requested, "May I see what he has done?"

"Mainly, he left a mess," Tiffany told her. "Right

now, if you saw it, you'd probably be horrified." And she had no desire to listen to her mother criticize what she saw. Why Tiffany felt almost protective of the man who had jolted her out of her bed was beyond her, but it didn't change the way she felt. "Why don't you wait until he's finished and then I'll show you just what he managed to do."

Much to her astonishment, her mother smiled and nodded. "I can hardly wait."

Tiffany wondered if Mei-Li was getting more eccentric as she got older—or if she was just becoming strange.

Tiffany found herself leaning toward the latter.

Chapter Four

"I thought women liked to go shopping," Eddie said, in response to the less-than-pleased expression on his passenger's face.

True to his word, he had arrived at eight in the morning. And as per their agreement, he had gone straight to work on the master bath, preparing it for the items he hoped they would wind up purchasing later today. That allowed Tiffany to get back to bed—downstairs in the guest room—temporarily.

Back to sleep, however, was another story. She couldn't seem to fall asleep because she kept waiting for the noise to begin.

It didn't. However, the ensuing quiet didn't allow her to drift off. After a while, Tiffany gave up her futile quest for sleep and got ready for the trip she told herself she didn't want to make.

They'd left at a few minutes after ten, with her looking less than pleased about the forced field trip she was facing.

"I do like to go shopping," Tiffany said when the silence became too uncomfortable. "I like to go shopping for clothes, for shoes. I even like to go shopping for electronic gadgets that I don't need but that capture my attention."

She shifted slightly in the passenger seat. Her seat belt dug into her hip. "But I have never even *once* fantasized about going shopping for bathroom faucets, or showerheads, or medicine cabinet mirrors."

"Then this should be a new experience for you," he told her cheerfully.

Tiffany caught herself thinking grudgingly that he had a nice smile, but she didn't exactly appreciate the fact that the smile was at her expense.

"And a quick one, I hope," she retorted.

"That all depends on you." For her benefit, Eddie went over the list of various hardware and fixtures needed in her bathroom, concluding with, "You find ones that you like and we'll be on our way back to your house in no time."

"What's the catch?" she asked.

Eddie shook his head as he guided his truck onto the freeway ramp. "No catch."

"Then why aren't we on our way to O'Malley's Hardware, or One Stop Depot?" she asked, naming two local hardware stores in the area that boasted having everything a home owner might need.

Taking advantage of a space, Eddie merged into the middle lane. "Because I'm assuming that you want quality, not shoddy." After he resumed the acceptable freeway speed, he spared Tiffany a quick look. "At least, that was what I was told by the person who hired me."

"O'Malley's Hardware sells shoddy goods?" she questioned.

Tiffany wasn't all that familiar with the store, only the ads that seemed to pop up every hour on most of the television stations. Even the jingle had begun to infiltrate her brain on occasion.

"They sell 'make-do' goods," he told her. "The stores I'm taking you to carry higher-end items that are made to last."

"And higher prices," she guessed.

Eddie nodded. "You get what you pay for," he told her simply.

She had a feeling that he was conveniently omitting one little fact. "And you get a percentage of all those high-end prices, right?"

She thought she saw him stiffen ever so slightly, as if he'd just taken offense. "I'm charging for my work," he pointed out. "The price—the *actual* price—of any fixtures gets passed on to your mother. You're welcome to take a look at the bills of sale if you want to."

She wasn't going to bother beating around the bush. "Then you don't increase the price of each item?" Tiffany challenged.

He shook his head. "That's not the way I do it," Eddie told her, although he doubted she believed him. But he had no intention of trying to convince her. She could believe him or not, that was her prerogative. He had better things to do than to try to prove his trustworthiness.

Tiffany shrugged her shoulders indifferently.

"Let's just get this over with," she told him with a deep sigh. Maybe he was actually telling the truth, maybe he wasn't. She just didn't want to waste any more time over this than she had to.

It surprised her how many choices there were of absolutely *everything* and how many stores were devoted exclusively to just one or two types of items. It was like entering a completely different world.

Although she had initially just wanted to point and go, Tiffany was stunned to find herself deliberating. Specifically, she was having a hard time picking out the kind of bathtub she wanted and exactly what she wanted built into it.

Out of the corner of her eye, Tiffany caught a glimpse of her "guide" in this gleaming fixture jungle, smiling to himself as she vacillated between two different models.

"You tricked me, didn't you?" she accused with only a slight frown.

Eddie spread his hands wide, the picture of total innocence. "I'm just the one who brought you here," he told her. "You're the one who's trying to decide between two kinds of bathtubs."

"Which I wouldn't be doing if you hadn't shown them to me," Tiffany pointed out, exasperated that she had been put in this position.

Eddie took the blame graciously. "Ah, but think what you would have been missing out on if we hadn't come here," he said.

Tiffany's eyes narrowed as she glared at him. "You can't miss what you don't know," she countered stubbornly.

The expression on his face all but told her that he knew she didn't believe that, even though, out loud, he made it sound as if he was capitulating. "Whatever you say."

Tiffany realized they were going to stand here in this little shop until she came to some sort of a decision. With a huff she pointed to the tub that came loaded with top-of-the-line Jacuzzi features.

"That one," she announced. "I'll take that one."

Looking solemn, Eddie nodded. "Good choice." And then he stopped her dead in her tracks as he asked in a very mild voice, "What color?"

Completely frustrated, Tiffany threw up her hands. "Arrgh!"

"I don't think it comes in that color," he replied evenly. "How about light blue?"

For some strange reason, the man was enjoying this. She could have strangled him.

"Fine." Tiffany bit off the word. "Get the bathtub in light blue."

The corners of his mouth curved. "See how easy that was?"

Her fingers began itching again. She would have loved to wrap them around his neck. "You're lucky that I'm not strangling you," she informed him from between clenched teeth.

"That *would* be extra," he told her, referring back to her earlier comment about his marking up the prices of everything that was bought in these smaller shops.

Tiffany closed her eyes, searching for strength.

"Can I go home now?" Tiffany asked, once the tub had been written up and a deliver date finally agreed upon.

"Not yet, but you're almost done," the contractor told her in a soothing voice as he ushered her out of the store. The truck was just a few feet away in the parking lot.

"Almost" took another two hours.

But finally, after what felt like an eternity to Tiffany, all the necessary choices for the next wave of remodeling had been made and the orders had all been placed, with specific instructions for delivery.

Since she couldn't be there during regular hours because she was teaching—there was no way she would be able to take off time to sit around waiting for fixtures to appear—her sisters were going to take turns staying at her house, waiting for most of the items to be delivered—with the exception of the toilet and the sink. Those had been firmly secured in the flatbed of the truck and were coming with them.

"Nice system," Eddie told her, complimenting her on the way she was able to get her family to pitch in and pick up the slack for her.

Tiffany's tone was icy as she replied, "Glad you approve."

Eddie was oblivious to her tone. He was focusing instead on what he would be getting paid for this remodel and the fact that it would help him pare down his once painfully bloated student loan even more.

"If it matters," he told her calmly, "this is the fastest that any client I've worked with has ever made their selections."

She wanted to say that it didn't matter at all, but in all honesty, she couldn't. Tiffany would be the first to admit that she had been born with a highly developed competitive streak, and reveled in being the best at everything, no matter how small or insignificant the challenge.

As far back as she could remember she always had to be at the top of her class, the one who finished tests first, who knew the answers before anyone else did. Even the first to turn in a term paper. It was just the way she was—driven.

"Really?" she asked, trying to sound indifferent to what he was saying and failing miserably.

"Really," he told her with as much solemnity as he could muster.

Tiffany glanced at her watch and noted that it was almost one thirty. She did a quick calculation in her head. There was a little time to spare.

"Hey, would you like to stop somewhere for lunch?" she asked, feeling suddenly very magnanimous.

She didn't expect the answer she got.

"Can't. I've got a sink and toilet to install," he told her. If he noticed her jaw all but dropping open, he didn't show it. "I know you're anxious for this project to be over," he explained.

"Right. I am," she answered, recovering. She felt oddly let down, even though everything he said was absolutely right.

The next moment she told herself she was relieved. She'd almost made a stupid mistake, getting too close to someone who was working for her even though he was getting paid by her mother.

"Besides," she said, addressing the windshield instead of him, "I don't know what I was thinking. I don't have time to go out for lunch. I've got some things I need to do to prepare for tomorrow."

He nodded. Eddie understood just where she was coming from, since once he was done here, he intended to do the very same thing and finish preparing for his new job tomorrow.

"Thanks for the thought, though," he told her.

"Sure. Any time I can't buy you lunch," Tiffany said wryly, "just let me know."

His mouth quirked in a quick smile. "I'll be sure to do that," he answered, doing his best not to laugh.

Eddie stayed until almost five o'clock. He'd hoped to leave by three thirty, but ran into a plumbing problem while installing the new sink. Because he needed to put in a brand-new pipe, he had to make a quick run to the local hardware store for the right length of pipe, as well as an extra can of sealer.

Tiffany had promised herself to stay out of his way the entire time, and she did. But when the contractor made his run to the hardware store, her conscience finally got the best of her. As far as she could see, the man hadn't stopped to eat all day. So while he was gone, she took the opportunity to make him a quick ham and Baby Swiss sandwich with lettuce, tomato and a sliced pickle on a cheddar cheese roll.

Taking a can of diet soda out of the refrigerator— it was all she had—Tiffany carried the sandwich and soda to the master bathroom on a tray and left them on the floor next to the sink Eddie was working on.

Then she smiled to herself and retreated back to the room she had converted into an office. She closed the door just as she heard the contractor return.

"I'm back," he announced loudly, not wanting Tiffany to think some stranger had just walked into her house.

She remained in her office and made no acknowledgment that she'd heard him. Giving the man until the count of ten, she opened her door just a crack and then returned to her desk to work.

Except that her mind wasn't really on the lesson plan spread out on her desk. She was too busy listening to the contractor's movements.

She heard him go up the stairs and then, because a lot of the floorboards beneath her carpet creaked, she heard him walk into her bedroom. As she listened closely, he stopped abruptly.

Tiffany took that to mean that the contractor had seen the lunch she'd left for him. Either that or he'd walked right into it. If that were the case, she expected to hear a few ripe, choice words coming through the ceiling.

None came.

After a few minutes, she heard the sound of a drill being used. He'd obviously gotten back to work.

Time for you to do the same, she told herself with a sigh as she looked down at the lesson plan she was working on. Eleven-year-olds were sharper these days than she remembered them being when she was that age. Tiffany got along well with her students, but there was no doubt about it—she definitely had to be on her toes if she didn't want them overwhelming her.

Forty-five minutes later, Tiffany realized that although she was almost finished working on the week's lesson plan, part of her was listening for some sort of an indication that the contractor was leaving—

or had he already left? She'd been lost in thought for a while, so if he had walked across the bedroom and down the stairs, she wouldn't have heard him.

She was debating going upstairs to check when she heard a knock on her office door. Startled, Tiffany jumped.

Silently upbraiding herself for being so skittish, she called out, "Yes?"

"I'm leaving now," Eddie told her.

Since Tiffany had left her door ajar, he was slowly pushing it wider with the tips of his fingers. By the time it was fully open, she was on her feet and standing there.

"You finished putting in the sink, cabinet and toilet?" she questioned.

The smile on his face gave her her answer. "Would you like to see how they look?"

"Sure, why not?" she replied, trying her best to sound nonchalant. After all, it was only a bathroom, right? There was no reason to be excited about it— and yet that was just the word to describe how she was feeling.

"Just remember that it's a work in progress," the contractor told her as he led the way upstairs.

"You sound like I should be braced for the worst," she said.

"Not the worst," he replied. "But it's definitely not finished."

After walking into the bathroom ahead of her, Eddie stood off to the side and allowed her a clear view.

Tiffany looked around slowly. For some reason she couldn't explain to herself, she experienced a tinge of pride when she gazed at the fixtures she had been instrumental in selecting.

"Well, it looks better than it did this morning," she commented, doing her best to sound blasé. And then, because she could feel him watching her, she felt she had to say something a little more positive. "It looks nice." Turning toward him, she added, "The blue looks good in here."

"You picked it," he reminded her, taking absolutely no credit.

Tiffany nodded, pleased with the way it was all turning out. "Yes, I did, didn't I?"

Eddie glanced at his watch. Though part of him would have liked to remain a little longer, he couldn't. He still had work waiting for him at home. Tomorrow was a big day.

"Well, I'll see you next Saturday," he told her, walking back out into the hallway.

"At eight?" She was hoping for later, but by now she knew better.

He reached the stairs. "Earlier if you'd like."

The idea of getting up any earlier horrified her. "Oh no, eight's early enough."

He grinned at her comment. "That's what I thought." With that, he hurried down the stairs. Tiffany kept pace with him, so they reached the bottom at the same time. He had a feeling she would.

"Okay, I'll see you Saturday morning," he told her, and then, because in his hurry he'd almost forgotten, he stopped just short of the front door and looked at her over his shoulder. "And thanks for lunch. Best sandwich I've had in a long time."

She'd almost forgotten about that. "Oh. Yeah, sure.

I just threw some things together," she said in an off-hand manner.

Eddie smiled to himself as he hurried to his truck. She'd made an effort and he liked that. He couldn't help wondering what she'd say once she remembered who he was. *If* she remembered, he qualified, as he started up his engine.

Chapter Five

There was a clock radio with the customary built-in alarm next to her bed on her nightstand. But Tiffany never bothered setting it. For as far back as she could remember, she had hated the annoying sound of an alarm piercing the air, no matter what the time was. Being jarred out of a sound sleep was way down on her list of priorities.

In order not to rely on an alarm, she had trained herself to wake up several minutes before the alarm *would* have gone off if she had actually set it to the time she needed to be up.

That didn't mean she bounced out of bed fully awake, bright-eyed and bushy-tailed and ready to take on the world. Instead, at the appointed time Tiffany would sit up, still half-asleep and fervently wishing for a snowstorm that would necessitate closing down the school district—something that wasn't about to happen. Not just because she lived in Southern California, but because it was April, and a rather warm April at that.

"C'mon, up and at 'em," Tiffany mumbled this morning, giving herself what amounted to a half-hearted pep talk. "You'll feel better once you get into the shower."

And then she remembered. If she wanted that shower, she was going to have to go downstairs to get it, because while her sink and toilet were fully functional, her showerhead still didn't know the meaning of the word *water*.

"Wonder Man" hadn't managed to fully hook that up yet, she thought darkly.

If she were being completely fair about this, she had to admit that the contractor had done an awful lot given the time constraints and the fact that they had gone to pick out the items for the remodel together.

But still, what would it have taken to hook up the showerhead?

Obviously more than he'd had the time for, she thought grudgingly as she went down the stairs, carrying all the items she usually needed when she took a shower.

Her arms felt overloaded.

Tiffany sighed. She had a feeling it was going to be a long week.

It turned out that even with the out-of-the-way trek to the guest bathroom for that life-affirming shower, Tiffany still managed to arrive in her classroom fifteen minutes before her wisecracking, pubescent crew descended on her.

Standing in the empty room, she savored the silence. As a teacher, this was the time of day she liked the best. Mornings, before her students came filing in, trying to outshout one another, and jockeying for seats even though they wound up in the same ones every day.

Mornings, when everything was still fresh and new, and potential abounded just about everywhere.

From this vantage point, anything was possible and she reveled in those possibilities.

Tiffany paused to look out the window. The school yard was beginning to fill up with students. Her window faced the side of the building where the younger grades, one through three, would line up.

She taught fifth grade, but had a very soft spot in her heart for children in the first three grades. For the most part, they were still the epitome of innocence, still very open to learning and to accepting teachers as authority figures who led the way to a richness of knowledge.

A great many times that sort of attitude changed all too quickly—which was why, when she first began applying for a teaching position, she had turned down an offer to teach in high school. Even middle school seemed to have its share of jaded students, so she had gravitated toward elementary school. Fifth grade seemed like a good fit for her, but if she had to, Tiffany knew she wouldn't mind working with even lower grades than that.

There was a sweetness about the younger children, almost a—

Tiffany's mouth dropped opened as she spotted a familiar figure crossing the school yard. She stared, watching until he eventually turned a corner and was out of sight, no matter how she angled her head.

Was that—

Yes, it was.

It looked just like him.

It was the man who had spent this past weekend tearing apart her bathroom.

What was he doing here? And why, during that entire time, hadn't he mentioned anything about having a school-aged child?

Almost pressed against the bay window now, watching him as he came back into view, Tiffany scanned the area surrounding the contractor. None of the children appeared to be making eye contact with him. Or, for that matter, trying hard to avoid eye contact—because sometimes, having a parent with you on the school grounds was a source of embarrassment for a child, especially the ones who wanted to appear independent and cool.

Well, if he wasn't bringing a child to school, what was the contractor doing here? He looked too well dressed to be doing handiwork. Besides, they had two janitors on the premises. Anything that came up, even if it was out of the ordinary, the two were more than capable of handling. And any kind of major structural work was done during the summer, when the school was closed. But this building had just been opened last September, so was far too new to need anything like that.

So what…

As she ran out of options to explain the man's

presence, she saw the principal, a tall, Nordic looking blonde, walking up to him.

From where Tiffany was standing, the exchange
between the two appeared to be warm and friendly.

Did they know each other?

Were they dating?

And where were these overly personal questions
coming from? she silently demanded. Besides, the
two couldn't be dating. Ada Walters, the principal,
was happily married.

Then what…

The school bell rang and she heard a scurry of feet
as small children hurried to line up in the spaces designated for each class.

A few minutes later, the lines were filing in through
the school doors and down the halls—in many cases,
moving in a somewhat less than orderly fashion.

The school day was beginning.

Any questions she had about what the man her
mother had hired to remodel her bathroom was doing
on school grounds were going to have to wait until
at least lunchtime, the earliest chance she'd have to
catch a moment with the principal.

For the time being, she had twenty-eight young
minds to challenge and inspire—or at least some reasonable facsimile.

Rather than stopping in the principal's office
when lunchtime came, Tiffany found herself out in
the school yard, on the side designated for the higher
grades. She'd forgotten that she had drawn yard duty
this week—patrolling half the grounds with one of

the other teachers, making sure that no infringements happened.

Roughly translated, that meant that no one was bullying anyone else and that none of the kids were being precocious and attempting to experiment with students of the opposite sex. More than a few were curious to see what all the excitement was about when it came to things like reaching first and second base— and maybe a base more than that.

But for the most part, yard duty was usually uneventful.

However, the moment she saw Alisha Carroll heading her way, Tiffany knew that something was up today. She had never seen the other teacher, whom she had known for several years, look quite so excited before.

To save time—or so she thought—Tiffany decided to get the ball rolling by initiating the exchange. "Hi, what's up?"

"What's up?" Alisha echoed. A short, dark-haired woman with lively eyes and an animated smile, she looked as if she was going to burst if she didn't share what was on her mind in the next sixty seconds. "Did you see who they got to replace her?"

The question came out of nowhere, catching Tiffany totally unprepared. Alisha, she'd learned, had an unfortunate habit of starting sentences in the middle of a thought.

"Replace who?" Falling into step, Tiffany began to walk beside her friend.

"Who?" Alisha asked incredulously, staring at her as if she'd become simpleminded. "Why, Chelsea Jamison, of course."

Right. Tiffany had completely forgotten that the third-grade teacher had gone into labor last Wednesday—right in the middle of story time. Some of her students had watched the mini-drama unfold with rabid excitement, others had gone screaming for the principal, crying that "Mrs. Jamison is coming apart!"

All the students in the school had talked about nothing else for the rest of the week.

Tiffany nodded, getting back on track as they continued to walk around their side of the school yard. "That's right, her class was going to get a substitute to fill in. I take it they did."

"A substitute?" Alisha repeated, as if she found the word distasteful. "Lord, I hope not. I hope that he's here permanently." She sighed wistfully. "At least until the end of the school year. Hopefully longer than that."

"He?" Tiffany repeated, waiting to be filled in. Was the substitute teacher a male? So far, all the teachers at Bedford Elementary were female. She supposed that getting a male teacher on staff could be a reason for some excitement.

"Yes, *he*," Alisha said with more emphasis than Tiffany thought her friend would use. "You mean you haven't seen him yet?" she cried, surprised. And then she grinned. Widely. If it was possible for a person to have stars in her eyes, Tiffany decided, then that was what was happening in Alisha's. "Boy, are you in for a treat."

Her friend had to be kidding. The Alisha Tiffany knew was a stable, grounded woman. The one she was talking to bore next to no resemblance to that person. Alisha appeared almost awestruck.

"Alisha, you're married, remember?" Tiffany said with a laugh.

"I'm married, not dead," her friend pointed out. "Besides, there's no harm in looking—and drooling when the kids aren't watching," she added with another almost wicked grin.

Tiffany made her own judgment call regarding what the other teacher was saying. "So I take it that he's good-looking."

"'Good-looking?'" Alisha echoed. And then she nearly laughed out loud. "Honey, that's a paltry description. If you look up the term 'drop-dead gorgeous' in the dictionary, you'll find a picture of this guy. And he's *single*," she stressed, looking right at her.

"Good for him," Tiffany remarked casually. What was she supposed to say? Right now, she didn't feel as if she was in a place where the marital status of *any* man mattered to her.

Alisha stopped walking for a moment, fisting her hands and putting them on her hips as she insisted, "No, good for *you*."

Tiffany was more than familiar with that tone of voice and she intended to put a stop to where this conversation was going right now, before her friend could get any more carried away.

"Alisha, listen to me," she requested. "I am very happy just the way I am."

Alisha pursed her lips and shook her head. "No, you're not. You're *resigned* to the way you are. But not every guy's a lowlife like Neil," she insisted.

Alisha was one of the few friends actually privy to Tiffany's past, and obviously felt that gave her the right to attempt to orchestrate Tiffany's private life. That's what she got for sharing, Tiffany thought.

"You need to get out there," Alisha insisted. "To get back on the horse before you forget how to ride altogether."

It took effort not to roll her eyes. But there were students watching, so Tiffany managed to hold herself in check. "Thank you for your concern, Alisha, but I am not interested in getting back up on any horse *or* in riding. I am very happy with the way my life is."

"You mean dull?" her friend interjected.

Alisha might have meant well, but Tiffany was coming to the end of her supply of patience here. "You're beginning to sound like my mother, and she's already descended on me once this week. So I don't need another lecture on how empty my life is."

"But it *is* empty," Alisha stressed, quick to jump on the opening that she'd been provided.

Tiffany was not about to give in. "I have nieces and nephews and a classful of students. Trust me, my life is very full."

"No, you're just running from the truth," Alisha insisted.

"Right now the only one I'm running from is you," she informed her, abruptly turning on her heel and heading in the opposite direction.

She was so intent on putting some distance between herself and her annoying friend that she didn't see him until it was too late. When she did, Tiffany couldn't stop in time and walked smack into the man she knew to be her contractor.

It struck her, as she made jarring contact with his rock-solid frame, that she hadn't even bothered getting the man's name this weekend. She had his card, which had the name of his construction company and his phone number, but as far as she recalled, she hadn't bothered to turn the card over to read his name, or even if there was one printed on the back side. It hadn't been important to her at the time.

So rather than being able to say his name, or shout it like an accusation, all she could do as she took a step back was say "You."

"Yes," the school's new third-grade teacher responded, grabbing her by the shoulders to minimize the impact of their collision, "it's me."

"What are you doing here?" It occurred to her this was the second time in three days that she'd asked him that question. The man just seemed to keep popping up in her life when she was least prepared to see him.

"Right now, apparently keeping you from hitting the ground because you just walked into me. Looks like your hand-eye coordination might need a little bit of work," he observed.

Annoyed, Tiffany shrugged off his hands. "I wasn't going to fall," she informed him coldly.

Like a man who knew when to surrender, Eddie made a point of holding his palms up, away from her.

"My mistake," he responded. And then, dropping his arms to his sides, he smiled as he regarded her. "Tell me—are you always this waspish, or do I bring it out in you?"

"We'll go with that," she told him curtly, then asked again, "Why are you here?"

"Because your principal hired me to be here," he told her.

Tiffany was still not making the connection. Or maybe it was her brain, out of a sense of self-preservation, that just refused to put two and two together to get the obligatory four.

"To do what?" she asked.

He enunciated each word slowly, as if he was talking to someone who wasn't quick to pick up on things. "To teach."

Tiffany's brow furrowed. Inexplicably, she could feel her stomach sinking. "Teach what?"

"Whatever it is that third graders need to learn," he told her.

Her mouth dropped open just as the bell rang, ending lunch period and summoning the students back to their classrooms. "You're taking Chelsea Jamison's place?" she asked, dumbfounded.

"As adequately as I can, yes."

Tiffany felt he was mocking her, yet didn't back off. "But you're a contractor," she protested.

"Among other things, yes, I am," he agreed, as he began to head back toward the building's side door. "But that isn't my main career," he told her, pausing to hold the door open for her.

Dazed, Tiffany didn't remember stepping past him, didn't remember walking into the building itself. Right now, she felt like Alice—sans the long blond hair—at the exact moment that the fictional character found herself tumbling down the long, winding rabbit hole.

Except that in her case, she didn't think there was any bottom to this unexpected opening in the ground.

As she put one foot in front of the other, reminding herself that she had a class to teach, she looked to her right and saw Alisha grinning broadly. The shorter woman was mouthing, *"See? Didn't I tell you he was gorgeous?"*

Tiffany blew out a breath. She didn't have time to absorb any of this.

Squaring her shoulders, she marched in the general direction of her classroom. With any luck, this was all a bad dream and she was going to wake up any minute now.

Chapter Six

It suddenly hit Tiffany out of the blue, somewhere in the middle of an impromptu spelling bee she'd decided to hold in her classroom to challenge her students. For no apparent reason, other than perhaps because Rita Espinoza, who was way ahead of the other girls in the class when it came to maturing, asked her, "If you have to be out for any reason, do you think that Mr. Montoya could substitute for you?"

Tiffany stopped dead and looked at Rita. The question had nothing to do with the last word she had just given one of the boys to spell. Several of the girls seated around Rita began to giggle.

Temporarily forgetting about the spelling bee, Tiffany tried to piece things together. "What name did you say?" she asked Rita in a very quiet voice.

Like a budding femme fatale, Rita tossed her long,

wavy black hair over her shoulder. "Mr. Montoya," she repeated. "You know, that new teacher."

"The one who's taking over Mrs. Jamison's third-grade class," another student, also a girl, volunteered.

"Lucky kids," Ellen Wallace said wistfully from the back of the classroom.

"He's not so great." Danny Quinn's reedy voice was joined by several other male voices that echoed the same sentiment, except possibly louder.

Any second now, Tiffany could see, an argument was going to break out. And *that* was what jostled her memory even more than the name Rita had just used. Because she and another student in her college classes—a male student going for a teaching degree just like she had been—used to lock horns in several classes on a regular basis.

Whether it was over practical teaching methods, or who was the better student in class, or who wrote the better paper—plus a thousand and one smaller, pickier things—they always wound up in a verbal sparring match.

It seemed that no matter what she did—whether it involved elaborate projects, term papers or student teaching jobs—somehow the other student would either match her or outdo her. Everything felt like a constant competition. She'd begun to feel like he was her nemesis. And *his* last name was Montoya.

Eddie Montoya.

Tiffany felt as if she'd just been struck by lightning.

Of course, why hadn't she realized that this weekend? There'd been this nagging feeling that she recognized the contractor from *somewhere. Knew* him from somewhere. But every time she tried to hone in on the elusive memory in order to pinpoint just where she knew him from, it managed to slip through the tiny slits of her mind, eluding her.

One reason for that was because the Eddie Montoya she remembered had been a great deal louder than the man she had spent part of the weekend with, pawing through tile samples and showerheads. This man was soft spoken.

The other, more obvious reason was that her archrival in college had had long, practically blue-black hair and a beard that Blackbeard the Pirate would have been proud of. There were times, after a particularly annoying verbal sparing match, when she'd actually fantasized yanking that beard out by its roots, hair by annoying hair.

The last day she remembered seeing the infuriating Montoya was at finals, just a week before they were to graduate from college.

But Montoya wasn't at the graduation ceremony. She'd heard, via the grapevine, that some family emergency had come up, taking him away and preventing him from attending graduation.

She'd told herself that she was greatly relieved not to have him there, but there was a part of her that had wondered just how serious an emergency it had been to keep him from something that she instinctively knew was so important to him.

But no one could tell her. Eventually, she forgot about Eddie altogether. She had a life to live and a career to pursue. She got engaged. She got unengaged. And good or bad, life always continued.

And now, suddenly, after not even crossing her

mind in over five years, Montoya suddenly turned up to haunt her school *and* her bathroom.

Talk about there being a crack in the universe, Tiffany thought disparagingly.

The next moment, she realized that she'd let her mind wander, and she roused herself. Because she'd temporarily drifted off, the noise level in her classroom was swelling.

"Settle down, class," she said in an authoritative voice she seldom used. "This is supposed to be a spelling bee, not an infestation of angry wasps. *Class,*" she repeated with more force, when the noise level remained around the same decibel.

It was the male contingent that looked at her sheepishly rather than the girls.

"Sorry, Ms. Lee." Curtis Choi, one of the boys sitting closer to the front of the room, apologized for his male brethren.

"Apology accepted, Curtis." She succeeded in keeping the smile from her lips as she looked at her class. "Can anyone here tell me Mr. Montoya's first name?"

Several of the girls' hands shot up, waving at her eagerly.

Big surprise there, Tiffany thought.

"Bethany?" She nodded at Rita's best friend. Apparently friends believed in sharing the wealth, and in this case, that meant information about the handsome new teacher.

"Mr. Montoya's first name is Ed," Bethany volunteered.

"No, it's not," Linda Clark declared, "it's Eddie."

"Eduardo." A third girl, June Garcia, corrected the other two with a haughty air.

This could definitely turn ugly, Tiffany thought. The girls were beginning to sound territorial.

"Those are all variations of the same name, girls," she pointed out.

"Who cares?" Gerald Goldsmith asked in disgust, slouching in his seat.

Gerald was languishing away his entire fifth-grade existence with braces affixed to both his upper and lower teeth, and resented anyone who could say something without having metal flash and people around him flinch.

"Ms. Lee cares." Another girl, Debbie, spoke up as if to defend her.

Tiffany raised her voice until she got the others to stop talking. "Just trying to gather information, class, that's all—and all of you seem to be so well informed." She eyed them pointedly. "I hope that you're half this informed on Friday when I give you that history quiz."

For the first time all day, her class did something in unison. They groaned.

Reminiscent of her own elementary school days, Tiffany found herself counting the minutes until the dismissal bell finally rang. The second it did, she waited impatiently for her class to file out.

Ordinarily, they all but flew out the door. But today, for some reason, some of her students seemed to take an inordinate amount of time getting their books together before leaving.

The moment they were out, so was she, making her

way along the serpentine hallway until she reached what had been, until last Wednesday, Chelsea Jamison's classroom. She wanted to corner Eddie Montoya and ask him exactly what sort of a game he thought he was playing, turning up at her school like this—especially with no warning.

But when she got to his classroom, it was empty. Both the man she had once regarded as the thorn in her side and the classroom of third graders he had taken over were missing.

She stood there for a moment, looking into the room, thinking that maybe if she waited long enough, Montoya would turn up, because he'd left something behind, or needed to check something before he went home. Or wherever it was that he went.

But the classroom remained empty, mocking her with its silence.

"If you're looking for the new stud, take a number."

Startled, Tiffany swung around to see Jill Hailee, one of the two kindergarten teachers, passing by. The woman stopped beside her. "Talk is that all the single teachers are drawing lots for who gets first crack at the guy."

"I don't want a crack at him," Tiffany retorted— which wasn't technically correct. She did want to take a crack at him, but not in the way that the kindergarten teacher meant. She wanted to give him a piece of her mind for playing a dirty trick on her— or whatever it was he thought he was accomplishing by pretending he didn't know her. "I just wanted to ask him a question."

"Yeah, right." Jill laughed. "So do the others. You'd think that this was high school all over again," she stated, shaking her head. About to leave, Jill stopped for another moment and murmured, "Wonder how many times a week that guy hits the gym."

"The gym?" Tiffany repeated, confused.

"Yes, the gym," Jill stressed. "You don't get biceps like that in a box from Amazon."

The second she'd said that, Tiffany found herself trying not to think of glimpsing the man in her bathroom on Sunday afternoon. Because it had been hot, he'd worked up a sweat quickly. Less than half an hour into the job, he'd stripped off his shirt—and looked as if he'd stepped off the cover of a fitness magazine.

Shutting down the memory, Tiffany tried to redirect the conversation. "How would you know what his biceps look like? He was wearing a jacket," she reminded the other teacher.

Jill frowned. The kindergarten teacher looked at her as if she found her hopeless. "Because, unlike you, I am observant."

"And really imaginative," Tiffany couldn't help retorting.

She needed to get out of here—and to mentally regroup, Tiffany told herself. Right now, everything was beginning to sound insane to her—especially her fellow staff members.

As an afterthought, she said, "I'll see you tomorrow."

"Absolutely," Jill responded, an anticipatory grin on her face. "A herd of wild horses couldn't keep me away."

"Happy trails," Tiffany murmured, as she walked toward the nearest exit.

She wanted answers. Barring that, she wanted to get as far away from the school building as was humanly possible. At least until she cooled down enough to sound rational when she started asking questions.

Tiffany knew that if she marched into the principal's office right now, to find out just how Montoya's name had come up and why she had hired him to take over the third-grade class, she would undoubtedly come across as a harpy. That was *not* the way she wanted to present herself to Ada Walters.

Because if she did that, then sympathy would instantly be on Montoya's side. She'd seen that before, in college, and didn't want it to happen again. But eventually, she was going to get her answers—and then she wanted him gone.

It seemed a simple enough plan.

As she crossed the school yard to get to her vehicle, Tiffany scanned the area. The way she saw it, the yard, especially after hours, was fair territory.

But the so-called teacher-contractor was nowhere in sight.

She did have his business card, she remembered. But she'd be damned if she'd call him like some teenaged girl tracking down the high school hunk.

Where had that come from? Tiffany asked herself, startled.

Montoya wasn't a hunk, he was an annoyance. A five-foot-ten *huge* annoyance. The same way he'd been in college, needling her at every turn, challenging her every word. She'd spent half her college years trying to find a way to outdo him, to top him at his own game and put him in his place.

Despite her efforts, she never felt that it quite happened.

And now, just when she'd settled in at Bedford Elementary, happy with the space that she'd carved out for herself, Montoya had to come waltzing in. There was no doubt in her mind that he was going to ruin everything.

The universe hated her, she thought, feeling its full weight on her shoulders.

Half-formed thoughts came and went as she drove home, but nothing was resolved by the time Tiffany pulled up, disgruntled, in her driveway.

She'd come up with only one possible lead that might give her a clue as to why Montoya was turning up in her life after all these years.

Tiffany knew that following up on it might make her vulnerable, but she wanted an answer more than she wanted to hide. Focusing on her goal, she switched off the engine and got out of her car, not bothering to put it away in the garage. She had something more important to do right now and if she hesitated, she would lose her nerve.

The second she walked in through her door, she forced herself to call her mother.

It wasn't that she didn't love her mom—she did, a great deal. But unless she was in a bulletproof state of mind, Tiffany found it a lot easier just avoiding her.

But her mother was the only one who could answer her question, so Tiffany forced herself to press the single button on the keypad that would connect her to her mother's phone.

"Hello, Mom," Tiffany said, doing her best to sound cheerful. It had rung twice before she'd picked up.

Was that by design, or just by chance?

Tiffany fervently wished that they could have a normal relationship. Although, probably to her mother, this *was* normal.

"Hello. Is this my unmarried daughter?" she heard the woman ask.

"Wow, two seconds. That's a new record, even for you, Mom," Tiffany marveled.

"Record?" Mei-Li questioned, a note of confusion entering her voice. "I am not playing a record."

"They're called CDs now and no, you're not," Tiffany agreed. "I meant a new record for starting in on me about not being married."

"I did not start you not being married, Tiffany," she protested, somehow twisting the words to get them to say what she meant. "That is all your doing."

Tiffany sighed. *Calm, stay calm. You don't want to blow up.*

"I didn't call to talk about my nonmarital status, Mom," she said evenly. "I called to ask you where you found that contractor you sent over last Saturday to remodel my bathroom."

"I did not find him," Mei-Li told her in a dismissive tone.

Tiffany pressed her lips together. Sometimes her mother took things so literally it could make her scream. She struggled to hold on to her temper. Raising her voice would accomplish nothing.

"Let me ask you another way, Mom," Tiffany said, trying again. "Who gave you his name?"

"Maizie Sommers did."

She heard her mother pause on the other end of the line, and wondered if she was trying to get her words lined up correctly. It wasn't that Mei-Li was searching for a way to say it in English, because the option to communicate in Mandarin was on the table. Tiffany understood that language, plus several other dialects, well enough to get the general gist of whatever her mother might want to say to her.

"Is this Maizie Sommers a friend of yours, Mom?" she finally asked, when her mother continued to remain silent.

Mei-Li didn't really answer the question, and the response she gave sounded almost rehearsed. "Maizie Sommers is a Realtor who sometimes must use people to fix things in the houses she sells."

"And she recommended the man you sent to me," Tiffany concluded.

"Yes."

She could almost see her mother bobbing her head. "And that's all?" Tiffany questioned. She'd expected that there was more of a reason behind all this than her mother was admitting to. Mei-Li Lee might look like a simple little woman but she was as devious as they came.

"Why? What more would you like, Tiffany?" her mother asked in that half patient, half exasperated tone of voice that could always drive her and her sisters up the wall.

There was no point in trying to push this any further, at least not right now. Her mother had just passed on information, and most likely had had her friend find some way to verify that the man she was sending to her youngest daughter's house wasn't an escaped serial killer.

Beyond that, Mei-Li probably felt her work was done.

Still, this now made Tiffany's life miserable on two fronts. And she was stuck with both. She certainly couldn't do anything about Montoya at school, and he was only half finished with the work on her bathroom. If she sent him packing, she would have to find someone else to take over. Most likely, that someone else would charge more—and knowing her mother, she probably wouldn't pay for a new handyman, telling Tiffany that if she was so fussy, she could pay for the work herself.

She knew her mother.

Still, Tiffany needed to get this out of her system. She couldn't stop herself from saying, "Whether you know it or not, Mom, you opened up a can of worms."

"Worms? I did not open up any can with worms. They must have come from your pantry." Mei-Li clucked in disapproval. "This is what comes of not cleaning out your pantry properly, as I have told you to do more than one time."

This was unraveling quickly and Tiffany knew it wouldn't end well. "Gotta go, Mom. Thanks for the housekeeping update."

She sighed so loudly as she hung up, she was pretty

sure her next-door neighbor heard her. She found herself envying Gwen, whose parents were retired and enjoying themselves traveling around the world. Gwen hardly ever heard from them.

"Lucky woman," Tiffany murmured.

Chapter Seven

Determined to enrich his students' learning experience, Eddie made sure that he got to school early the next morning. The halls were still empty when he went in.

His arms were laden with books he'd bought last night at one of the last remaining bookstores in the area, so he used his elbow to press down on the latch and open the door. Then he pushed it wide with his back.

Once inside his classroom, he turned around and almost dropped the books on the floor. He managed to catch himself at the last minute.

Due to the early hour, he hadn't expected to find anyone in the classroom. He *especially* didn't expect to find Tiffany standing there, given what he'd learned about her trying to sleep in until the very last second she could.

One look at her face told him that the woman was loaded for bear.

Bracing himself, Eddie made his way to his desk. He deposited the books on it and asked in the most cheerful voice he could summon, "Good morning, Ms. Lee. What can I do for you?"

She wasn't taken in by his tone, his politely worded question or the fact that he had referred to her as "Ms. Lee," something he hadn't done even this weekend when he'd first turned up on her doorstep—the underhanded rat. This was college all over again, Tiffany thought. Competition 101.

Her eyes narrowed as she glared at him. "You can tell me why you *didn't* tell me who you were."

Eddie was the soul of innocence as he replied, "You know who I am. I'm your contractor, the man your mother hired to remodel your bathroom."

"You know what I mean," she insisted, daggers all but shooting from her eyes.

Eddie began arranging the books on his desk alphabetically, creating several stacks as he went along. "I'll let you in on a secret," he told her. "Half the time in college, I didn't know *what* you meant."

There was that smile he probably thought was so disarming, Tiffany thought, growing angrier by the second.

"I've got a feeling that you didn't know, either," he concluded.

"Your name," Tiffany said through gritted teeth. She was *not* going to let him distract her. "Why didn't you tell me your name?"

"Why didn't you ask?" Eddie countered.

Picking up the first stack of books, he walked to

the back of the classroom, where a bookcase with two shelves ran along the wall. It was only partially filled with books, which was what had prompted him to go shopping for third-grade reading material.

It wasn't the first time he'd undertaken this kind of a mission. Books had always struck him as being magical, able to stimulate childrens' imaginations and transport them to different places and different times. By buying extra books, he wanted to inspire his new students to read on their own time.

"I gave you a business card," he pointed out, as he put the books on a shelf.

"It had the name of your company and your business phone number on the front. I'm talking about your actual name," Tiffany insisted. "That wasn't on there."

He gave her a tolerant smile. "All you had to do was turn the card over. Judging by your combative attitude," he said, making his way back to his desk to get another stack of books, "I take it you never did that."

She hadn't. She hadn't been interested enough in the intrusive contractor to turn it over, at least not that first morning. As a matter of fact, she really didn't remember where she had put the business card after he'd handed it to her.

Exasperated, Tiffany blew out a breath. She'd thought that he'd be done working in two days and she'd never lay eyes on him again. Unless she wanted something else reworked—excluding herself, she thought, knowing the kind of comment he probably would have made if he'd heard her say that.

How had this happened? Tiffany silently demanded.

"That is beside the point," she snapped. "You should have told me who you were."

Finished arranging the second stack of books, he returned to the desk to pick up the last stack and put them on the rear shelf alongside the others.

"You didn't recognize me?" Eddie asked, managing, at least for the most part, to keep a straight face. "I'm hurt."

Was he serious? Tiffany looked at him, stunned. "I didn't recognize you because back then you looked like some kind of a backwoodsman, or Blackbeard the Pirate." She waved a hand at him. The difference between then and now was like night and day. "You look civilized now."

He glanced up from the books he was putting away, surprised. "I take that as a compliment."

Tiffany frowned. "It wasn't meant as a compliment. It was meant to point out that you were disguised then—or disguised now. I don't know which," she told him, frustrated. "But whatever you were or are, you looked completely different, so there was no way I could have recognized you."

He glanced in her direction. "I got that part," he said in a calm voice. "What I don't get is what you're so angry about." Finished with the books, he made his way back to his desk.

She was right behind him.

"Because…" she began, then found she didn't have anything logical she could use in her defense. It wasn't as if he had taken advantage of her somehow, or capitalized on the fact that she hadn't recognized him. It was just that she felt she had been caught at a disadvantage and it made her feel like a fool, something she knew he enjoyed doing.

She said as much to Eddie, adding, "I feel like you're laughing at me."

He had begun to rearrange his desk. Pausing, he glared at her, his eyes meeting hers directly. "Do I look like I'm laughing?" he asked her softly.

What *was* it about this man that got to her this way? That made her temper flare and her blood pressure rise? They couldn't be in the same room for more than a couple minutes before she could feel it starting.

"You know what I mean," she muttered.

Eddie laughed drily, shaking his head. "Ah, so we're back to that again."

She was fuming and she couldn't even put into words why. But kicking him in the shin might have helped make her feel better—juvenile, but better.

"If you were a decent person, you'd go to the principal right now and tell her that—that…" Tiffany was almost sputtering. Words were failing her. Words *never* failed her. What was this man doing to her?

"And tell her what?" Eddie asked, still keeping his voice maddeningly level. "That we know each other? The fact that we do—or don't—doesn't have any bearing on my getting this position," he pointed out. "It's not as if you secretly found a way to have Mrs. Jamison go into labor early so that I could take her place."

He was right. Infuriatingly right. And Tiffany resented him for it.

Moreover, she had no idea why she felt the way she did about this turn of events. It wasn't as if Montoya and she were in competition for the same position—or even for who was the better teacher. She was teaching fifth grade and he had been brought in to take over a third-grade class. Feeling like this wasn't logical.

She didn't feel like being logical.

"You still could have told me who you were and that you were coming here."

The corners of his mouth curved even further. "Well, hypothetically, given the way you just reacted, maybe I didn't want to take a chance on getting you really upset and reacting the way you just did," he told her philosophically. "Besides, I didn't know you taught here when I accepted the assignment.

"Frankly," he added, choosing to be honest with her for a moment in hopes that might calm things down, "things have been a little rough lately. There were cutbacks at the last school where I taught. I was grateful for any job."

"Is that why you're remodeling bathrooms?" she asked.

Eddie tended to think of it in broader terms. "That's why I'm a contractor taking *any* job that comes my way."

Tiffany was still rather dubious about the whole turn of events. "So you remodeling my bathroom and then coming to work at my school… That all just happens to be a coincidence?"

"I can tell by the sarcasm that you're mocking me," Eddie replied, amused rather than angry, "but it's exactly that. Call it coincidence, a curse, or any one of a number of those kind of things. *Anything* but deliberate," he stressed. "Because, to be very honest, four years of sparring with you, of putting up with that razor tongue of yours every time we were around one another, was more than enough to qualify me for sainthood. Trust me, I wouldn't have knowingly sought you out."

That had to be a crock, she thought. Did he expect her to believe him? Did he think she was stupid? "So you didn't know who I was when you accepted the remodeling job?"

Eddie pointed out the obvious to her. "Well, if you think about it, it's not as if you have this really unique name."

She was not about to drop this. She wasn't buying his innocent act. "But once you saw me..." Tiffany said, pinning him with a look, daring him to deny that he didn't recognize her.

Eddie just spread his hands wide as he shrugged. "Hey, there are a lot of pretty girls named Tiffany out in the world."

She almost believed him. Almost, but not quite. "So you *didn't* know me, didn't recognize me?"

Eddie sighed. The woman was like a pit bull. A cute, dark-haired, blue-eyed pit bull that would not let go.

"Let's just say that I didn't at first, and once I did realize who you were, I had already put some work in on your bathroom." He tried to appeal to her logic, although part of him thought that was pretty much a lost cause. "I needed the job, you needed a bathroom, and since you didn't recognize me, there didn't seem to be any harm in my staying on."

"And now that I do recognize you?" Tiffany challenged.

He was not going to allow her to get to him, and definitely not going to allow her to make him lose his temper. He had a class coming in at any moment and he wanted to be in the right frame of mind for them.

"And now," he told her, "as far as I'm concerned, there's still no harm in it."

Tiffany opened her mouth, ready to state all her objections to his view of the situation. But the next second, she realized that she was going to have to table whatever she was about to say. She heard the bell ring, signaling the beginning of another school day.

The sound almost startled her. She'd spent so much time going back and forth with Montoya over what he insisted on saying was "nothing," getting absolutely nowhere.

So what else is new? Tiffany taunted herself. This was reminiscent of so many run-ins she'd had with him when they were in college.

Except that she was older and wiser now.

"This isn't over yet," she informed him, a crisp edge to her voice.

Eddie inclined his head. He expected nothing less. "I'm sure it's not."

There was a cocky grin on his face. Or maybe given the fact that they were older now, that look could be referred to as "confident."

Whatever the label for it, she wanted to scratch that grin off his face—which made her come off as irrational, she thought, resenting that Montoya had this effect on her.

But even so, she knew she would have felt a great deal of satisfaction if she'd given in to her desire.

Maybe next time, she told herself.

Squaring her shoulders, Tiffany turned and marched out of his classroom.

"Good talk," Eddie called after her.

For just a heated split second, she thought about lunging at him. But there would have been witnesses, so she didn't.

Leaving, she had to sidestep his students filing into the classroom, all looking very happy and eager to be there. And Montoya was obviously the reason for that.

Tiffany stifled a cryptic comment that came to her lips.

It was as if Bedford Elementary had just gotten its very own Pied Piper, she thought grudgingly. Well, he wasn't some magical being who could lead the students off to a wondrous place. He was just a man with his size nine—give or take—shoes planted firmly on the ground. Nothing magical about him.

His students would all find that out for themselves soon enough, she promised herself.

It was just a matter of time.

Trying to calm down, Tiffany walked to her classroom. Why did he make her so infuriated? Why did he get under her skin like that? After all, it wasn't as if he was trying to show her up, or beat her out of her position. They taught different grades.

For heaven sakes, they were even on separate sides of the school building. If she played her cards right, she wouldn't even have to see him. After all, how often had she seen Chelsea Jamison when Chelsea was there, teaching that same class?

The thought should have comforted Tiffany. The fact that it didn't just caused her to feel more irritated than she already did.

Get ahold of yourself, Tiff. You've got fifth graders to enlighten and you know they're a lot more de-

manding and a lot sharper than a classroom of third graders. You've got the harder job here, she silently argued as she walked into her room.

Why didn't that raise her spirits?

She wasn't in competition with Eddie Montoya. More like, she was in competition with herself.

Today's Tiffany Lee had to be brighter, sharper, more entertaining than yesterday's Tiffany Lee. And tomorrow she had to be an even better version of herself than today. The classwork—and her students— demanded it.

"Omigod, you *knew* him?" Alisha cried the second they got within speaking distance after lunch.

Startled, Tiffany glared at the shorter woman. Still preoccupied, she hadn't seen Alisha coming at her until it was too late.

She looked at her now, less than pleased at this new turn of events. "How did you find out?" she demanded.

Alisha waved a dismissive hand. "You know there're no secrets around here," she said, sounding annoyed that the question was even being asked. "It's like the walls have ears."

"That is a stupid expression," Tiffany said, dismissing it. "Now, tell me how you found out that he and I knew each other." Her eyes narrowed. "He didn't tell you, did he?"

"I wish," Alisha answered wistfully. "No, the hunky Mr. Montoya and I haven't exchanged more than 'Hello.' But boy, can that man put a lot of emotion into that word," she told Tiffany with a low, soulful sigh.

Tiffany felt herself losing patience. She needed to know how the other woman had found out—and if there was any need for damage control, because who knew what kind of a story was making the rounds?

"I'm waiting, Alisha," she said, pinning her with a look.

Alisha appeared almost delighted to have stirred her up this way. After a moment, the woman took pity on her. "Simple. One of the kids in his class asked him if he knew you—I guess he must have seen you talking to his new teacher—and Mr. Montoya said yes, he did." Alisha's steely gaze bored straight into Tiffany like a laser beam. "You were holding out on me yesterday," she accused.

"No," Tiffany replied, "I wasn't. At the time we talked, I hadn't recognized him yet."

"Right." The expression on Alisha's round face was exceedingly skeptical. "How could you *not* recognize that face? All you had to do was see him once and it would be forever branded in the folds of your brain."

Tiffany sighed. She was tired of going over what felt like ancient history by now. "Because that face, when I knew him, was hidden behind a beard that looked like it was second cousin to a bramble bush. In addition, he had this long, wavy hair. He looked more like a biblical prophet than a future teacher."

Alisha didn't seem to hear the description, or if she did, she wasn't put off by it. Sporting a dreamy-eyed expression, she asked, "What was he like back then?"

Tiffany refrained from reminding Alisha—again—that she was a married woman. Instead, she answered curtly, "Annoying. Incredibly annoying."

Alisha surprised her by laughing skeptically. "Methinks the lady doth protest too much. Either that or you've incurred a head injury you forgot to tell me about."

"Tell you what," Tiffany said. "You pick the explanation." With that, she turned on her heel and started back to the building.

"Where are you going?" Alisha called after her.

Tiffany didn't bother turning around. Instead, she tossed the words over her shoulder. "I forgot something in the lunchroom."

"What?" Alisha raised her voice so that she could be heard.

"I forgot to stay there," Tiffany murmured under her breath, walking a little faster.

Chapter Eight

With no other options open, Tiffany made up her mind to make the best of the situation that presently faced her.

She intended to avoid Eddie Montoya as much as humanly possible.

Unfortunately, her plan turned out to be about as successful as trying to avoid air. Like air, for some reason, Bedford Elementary's newest teacher seemed to be everywhere. Their paths crossed in the school yard, in the lunchroom, in the halls as well as in the parking lot.

The bottom line was that the man proved to be completely unavoidable. And although logically she knew that they were not in any sort of a competition, she couldn't seem to shake the feeling that on some subconscious level, they actually were.

Tiffany wasn't able to put it into words, not even to herself, but she felt challenged by Eddie's very existence within an arena she had considered, until this Monday morning, as her own.

As far as teaching went, it was hard enough being one step ahead of her students in an effort to keep them interested and motivated. Feeling as if she had to be on her guard and alert against anything coming her way from this interloper had created a tension within Tiffany that she couldn't seem to overcome.

This was crazy. She had to get a grip on herself, she silently admitted. It wasn't fair to her students for her to be like this. If nothing else, she was short-changing them—and becoming an emotional wreck to boot.

She'd been giving herself this pep talk all during her drive to school. By the time she pulled up in the parking lot, she still hadn't resolved anything or found any inner peace.

With a sigh, she got out of her car and grabbed her oversize purse. Moving quickly—she wanted to reach the shelter of her classroom as fast as possible—she promptly caught the purse's shoulder strap on the driver's-side door. She automatically tugged on it, and in the blink of an eye, a flurry of papers fell out of her purse and rained down around her vehicle in the parking lot.

Tiffany bit off a frustrated curse, not wanting to be heard swearing out loud within any student's hearing.

"Here, let me help you with that."

She didn't have to turn around to know who the deep, resonant voice belonged to. It belonged to the reason why everything was going wrong these days.

"That's okay," she told Eddie, without looking in his direction. She squatted down and started picking up the renegade papers. "I've got this. I don't need any help."

Tiffany came very close to swatting away his hand when he didn't pull it back fast enough. She clasped the papers in a heap against herself.

And then the very last thing she expected happened. Eddie laughed.

When she looked at him, annoyed beyond words, he commented, "Same old Tiffany."

"What's that supposed to mean?" she demanded.

Despite her defensive posture, Eddie took her by the arm and gently but firmly helped her to her feet.

"It means that every time I'm around you, I can almost hear someone singing the lyrics, 'Anything you can do, I can do better.'"

Her eyes narrowed as she shoved the papers haphazardly back into her purse. He was talking about a classic musical that periodically made the revival rounds. It centered around a rivalry between Annie Oakley and Frank Butler. In it, Frank was the polished performer and Annie was the backwoods sharpshooter who bested him.

"Meaning you?" she retorted. Turning on her heel, she headed toward the building.

"No, meaning you." Eddie fell into step beside her. "I never saw us as competing against one another."

"Then I guess you must have slept through those four years of college."

"No," he answered mildly, "I worked very hard during those four years. For me the object was to get an education—and a degree. What was your objective?" he inquired.

Despite the fact that she tried to walk faster than him, Eddie got to the front entrance first and held the door open for her. His legs were longer, she thought grudgingly.

She swung around the moment they were inside the building, scanning the area quickly to make sure there was no one else within hearing range. Satisfied that there wasn't, she answered Eddie's question far more honestly than she thought he had addressed hers. "To beat the pants off you every single chance I got."

Eddie appeared unfazed as he asked her, "Why?"

In the heat of her exasperation, Tiffany almost slipped and told him. Told him that back then he had been regarded as the best, which meant that she was determined to beat him because she had to be the best at everything she set out to do.

She caught herself at the last minute, because saying that would have been flattering to him, and she didn't want to be guilty of that.

So instead, she tossed her head and crisply informed him, "If you'll excuse me, I have to get to class. I have to set up something."

"Need help?" he offered cheerfully. By all indications, Tiffany realized that she had managed to arouse his curiosity.

She blinked. He had to be kidding. "The day I ask you for any help is the day you should get out of the way, because there'll be four horsemen galloping through the streets," she informed him, then turned her back and hurried away.

Eddie watched her for a moment, the corners of his sensual mouth curving in an amused smile. And then he headed in the opposite direction. His students would be filing into the classroom soon, and if everything was going according to plan, he had permission slips to collect.

Tiffany managed to elude the man she considered to be the bane of her existence for the rest of the day. At least their paths didn't physically cross.

But even so, Eduardo Montoya had taken up residence in her brain. Thoughts and images of the man would pop up in her head at random times—the most *inopportune* times.

The upshot seemed to be that the more she tried not to think about him, the more she did.

Tiffany felt as if she'd somehow been cursed.

But as far as running into the man, her luck, for once, seemed to hold. So much so that she grew a little suspicious of the fact that, other than in the parking lot that morning, she hadn't seen him the entire day.

Unable to suppress her curiosity, once the school day was officially over she made her way to Eddie's side of the building. Passing by his classroom, she peeked in as nonchalantly as possible.

The room was empty.

Neither Montoya nor a single child was there.

Something was up.

According to a couple of the other teachers, for the last three days surprisingly devious little girls had been finding all sorts of excuses to linger in Montoya's classroom once the day was over. And even his male students seemed inclined to hang around him when they didn't have to. Alisha had overheard two of the boys saying that they thought the new teacher was "cool."

At almost lightning speed, with apparently no effort, Eddie Montoya had become the male model all the little boys wanted to emulate.

So just where was this "cool" teacher now, and if his students liked to hang around after the dismissal bell had rung, why had his room emptied out so fast?

It didn't make sense, Tiffany thought as she turned away.

About to leave, she narrowly avoided bumping into the school janitor.

"If you're looking for Mr. Montoya, he took the class on a field trip," the man in gray coveralls told her. Leaning on a mop that was propped in its bucket, he was apparently waiting for her to vacate the area so he could clean the floor.

"A field trip?" That didn't sound right to her. "Are you sure? I didn't hear about any field trip being planned," Tiffany said.

"I guess that's 'cause it was a last-minute thing, kinda like hiring him on. He took the class to visit Mrs. Jamison and her new baby."

Tiffany stared at the stout, gray-haired man, stunned. "When did all this happen?" she asked. Nobody had said anything about visiting the new mother. She would have heard about it. She wanted to go visit Chelsea herself, but was giving the other teacher two weeks to get used to her situation and get a little rest—if that was even possible for a new mom.

"Today," the janitor told her. "He got Principal

Walters to sign off on it. I hear she even put up part of the money for the bus," the man marveled.

Something was definitely off. "But Montoya can't just take off with a classroom of kids," she protested. "There are permission slips to collect."

Archie grinned. "Saw him carrying a stack of those to Principal Walters's office this morning. Guy's right on top of everything." There was no missing the admiration in the janitor's voice.

Another true believer, she thought darkly.

"Right," Tiffany responded automatically, then echoed, "On top of everything."

What the hell was Montoya really up to? As far as she knew, he didn't know Chelsea Jamison, or Chelsea's husband, for that matter. So why was he going out of his way to make this so-called field trip happen?

Tiffany pressed her lips together. It didn't make sense to her and she didn't like anything that didn't make sense.

Most of all, she didn't like Montoya being glorified and regarded as the best thing that ever happened since low-calorie ice cream.

Not her business, Tiffany silently insisted. If the principal had sanctioned this, then so be it. There wasn't anything here that concerned her.

She'd almost managed to convince herself by the time she walked out to the parking lot and was about to get into her car.

And then she saw that Montoya's car was still parked in the lot. There were several other vehicles as well, belonging to teachers who had opted to remain after hours to catch up on their work.

If his car was there, that obviously meant he had to come back to get it.

Suddenly, she wanted to hear his explanation for all this.

Getting into her car, Tiffany pushed the driver's seat all the way back and made herself as comfortable as possible. Her objective was to conduct a stakeout.

She sat there, trying to keep her mind on the lesson plan she was drawing up, and listening for the bus to return to the lot. It struck her as strange that none of the third graders' parents was pulling up. Usually, whenever there was a field trip, there would be a glut of cars, complete with impatient parents, filling the parking lot.

But in this case, no cars and no parents appeared.

This whole venture was getting really strange.

Did the parents even *know* that he had taken their children off the school grounds on some impromptu field trip? Maybe he'd forged those slips the janitor claimed to have seen, and was off somewhere with those kids—

"And doing what?" Tiffany abruptly demanded out loud.

This wasn't some twisted made-for-TV movie. This was Montoya doing this, and as annoying as she found the man, she knew for a fact that he did like kids, liked teaching them.

So what was going on here?

Distracted, annoyed and deeply concerned, Tiffany had barely finished putting together the sketchiest of lesson plans for the following day when she saw the school bus pulling into the parking lot.

It's about time. She tossed her pad on the passenger seat.

Bracing herself, Tiffany was prepared to wait until all the students had gotten off the bus before confronting Montoya and demanding to know what the hell he thought he was doing, bringing a bunch of seven- and eight-year-olds to see an exhausted new mother.

But there weren't any students getting off the bus. As she watched, astonished, the only figures to emerge were the driver and his lone passenger.

The latter got off, saying a cheerful, "Thanks, David," before he began walking to his car.

Montoya.

Tiffany was out of hers like a shot and hurried over to Eddie before he had a chance to get to his own vehicle.

"Where are your students?" she demanded without any preamble.

He looked at her in surprise. "Tiffany, what are you doing here?" he asked. And then he grinned. "Are you waiting for me?"

She refused to answer outright. Instead, she repeated, "Where are your students? What did you do with them?"

He stared at her for a moment, as if he couldn't believe she was asking that question. "I didn't do anything with them. They're all home."

"You didn't take them on a field trip to Chelsea Jamison's house?" she pressed, exasperated.

"Well, yeah, I did. But then I dropped them off at their houses. Well, actually, I didn't." Half turning, he jerked a thumb in the bus driver's general direction. "David did."

She had the feeling that Montoya was toying with her. This was college all over again. "I don't understand," she told him, her voice growing progressively more agitated. "I don't understand any of it."

He spread his hands wide, as if at a loss as to what her problem was.

"Not much to understand," he told her. "The kids really wanted to see Mrs. Jamison. After what happened in the classroom last week, a lot of them said they were worried about her and wanted to see for themselves that she was all right. Some of the girls also expressed a desire to see the baby. So I called her yesterday morning to tell her that her class was asking after her—I figured hearing something like that would lift her spirits—and I asked if she was up for a *really* short visit from the kids, because they missed her and wanted to see her new baby.

"She told me she'd love to see them. I cleared it with the principal, printed up the standard permission slips and told the kids that they needed to have their parents sign them if they wanted to visit Mrs. Jamison and her baby."

Tiffany felt as if her head was reeling. "Just how the hell did you get permission for that?" she asked.

She watched as a dimple appeared in his cheek, the one that surfaced whenever his smile deepened. "Well, actually, when I told her, Ada thought that it was rather sweet."

Ada, Tiffany thought. *He's been here for four days and he's calling the principal by her first name. Even I don't call her that.*

Tiffany felt as if she'd woken up in a parallel universe.

"And the bus?" she asked. "Just how did you manage to get a bus on such short notice?"

Eddie lifted a shoulder, then let it drop dismissively. "I know someone who knows someone, and they pulled a few strings. Ada is paying next to nothing for the bus."

The man was nothing short of a magician. Even so, Tiffany still wanted to strangle him. "You actually took all those kids to see that poor woman," she said in disbelief.

"Best medicine in the world," he countered. "She looked a little down when she opened the front door, but once those kids started talking, telling her how much they missed her and how happy they were to see her, she perked right up." Though he didn't say it, Tiffany could see that he was proud of himself for bringing this about. "She really misses them," he said with empathy. "And she was touched that they were so worried about her. I'm glad I could bring them to see her. It was a win-win situation."

It was time for Tiffany to leave. "I guess you can add a Boy Scout merit badge to your résumé."

"That wasn't my intent," Montoya told her. There was no false modesty in his voice; it was just a statement of fact.

She made no acknowledgment one way or another, other than to grunt. Turning away, she went back to her car and got in without once looking in his direction.

A moment later, she was putting as much distance as she could between herself and the person she considered to be the most annoying man on earth.

Chapter Nine

The sound finally pierced through the heavy fog of sleep enshrouding Tiffany's brain. When it did, she stared, for the most part unseeingly, at the digital clock on the nightstand.

The numbers eventually registered.

That has to be wrong. The message telegraphed itself to her barely awake brain.

But even as the time slowly soaked in, the ringing sound continued, alternating with someone knocking on her door.

After groggily making her way to an upright position, Tiffany somehow wound up falling out of bed as she reached for a robe to throw over the football jersey she slept in.

That woke her up. Uttering a few choice words, she got up off the floor and tugged on the robe, which was in reality shorter than the extra-large jersey. She stretched out one foot, in search of her slippers. Coming up with nothing, she gave up and went out of her bedroom barefoot.

She really wished the doorbell would stop ringing, she thought angrily as she slid one hand along the banister and made her way down the stairs to the front door.

By the time she reached it she was not only fully awake, she was fully angry, as well.

All set to bite the guilty party's head off, she swung open the door.

Standing on her front step, Eddie looked at her disapprovingly. "You didn't ask who it was."

"I was hoping it was a burglar who'd put me out of my misery because someone keeps insisting on destroying my weekends," she growled. She stepped back, letting him in, although she wasn't entirely sure why she was doing that. She would much rather have just slammed the door in his face. "I didn't think you'd come back," she told him. Her robe fell open as she dragged a hand through her hair in a futile effort to get it to settle down.

His eyes swept over her for a split second, then politely looked away. He'd never seen a football jersey looking quite that sexy before. He wondered if it belonged to an ex-boyfriend.

"I didn't finish the job," he pointed out. "Why wouldn't I be back?"

Did he want her to spell it out for him? "Because now that you're the darling of Bedford Elementary and have practically everyone eating out of your hand, there's no need to continue at your 'side' job."

He paused at the foot of the stairs to look at her, deliberately focusing on her eyes. "You are so far from 'getting me' that it's mind-blowing," he told her.

With that, Eddie turned back toward the stairs, hefting his significantly large toolbox as he went up the steps to the master bathroom.

Tiffany was not about to let his sentence just hang like that in the air. She was right behind him. "Well, then enlighten me."

Eddie kept walking. "I start a job, I finish a job no matter what. It's as simple as that."

Reaching the landing, she sighed loudly, as if with every fiber of her being. "There is *nothing* simple about you."

Something in her voice definitely piqued his interest. Sparing her a glance over his shoulder, he grinned as he said to her, "Would you care to elaborate on that?"

She frowned. It was far too early for her to be able to coherently cite particulars. "No."

He shrugged. "All right then," he told her, walking into the bathroom, "I'll get to work."

She still didn't understand why he had come back. She'd heard more than one horror story about contractors who never returned to finish jobs they had started, either because they had gotten a better, more profitable opportunity, or because they had bitten off more than they could chew and couldn't properly finish the work. Montoya had a very plausible reason for not finishing her bathroom, not the least of which involved that she'd gotten in his face yesterday. And yet here he and his toolbox were.

She would have said he'd come just to wake her

up and annoy her, but if that was the case, he would have been gone by now, and he gave no indication that he would be leaving anytime soon.

As she watched, Montoya began to set up shop again inside the master bath he was remodeling.

"You're really going to do it," she said, somewhat stunned.

Nodding, Eddie continued working. "Unless you want to fire me."

She closed her eyes and wistfully muttered, "With my whole heart and soul."

He stopped preparing the wall over the tub for the tile he was going to place there, and turned to look at her, waiting.

"But my mother hired you, so I can't fire you."

There was a thoughtful look on his face. "Is that all that's stopping you?"

"That," she allowed, "and the fact that I don't want to have to go downstairs every time I take a shower."

"I see." His expression didn't change and told her nothing. "Well, then I'd better get back to work," he said as he picked up the trowel.

"Yeah, you'd better," she murmured.

But rather than go downstairs the way he likely expected her to, Tiffany went to her closet to grab something to wear once she finished showering.

Except she couldn't find what she wanted to put on.

Her clothes were all either tightly jammed together or doubled up on hangers in the cramped space. Already irritated, Tiffany found that her patience was in really short supply. After trying to shove several uncooperative hangers to one side, and failing, she muttered, "Damn!"

Hearing her, Eddie stopped prepping the wall and poked his head out of the bathroom. "Something annoying you—besides me?" he asked curiously.

"Yes," she snapped. "This closet. It's so shallow, I can't find anything I'm looking for."

Leaving his work, Eddie came into the bedroom to get a better look at what seemed to be causing her such angst.

The house had been built in the early seventies, and although it was nicely done and for the most part well maintained over the years, at the time it was constructed, walk-in closets hadn't come off the drawing board for most people. Closets were only a little deeper than the length of the hangers that were hung on the poles.

"I can see the problem," he told her.

"Well, glad to know that you've got good vision," she cracked.

"After I finish remodeling your bathroom, I could do something about that," he told her, nodding at her open closet.

She was not about to paint herself into a corner and have this man come to her house weekend after endless weekend. "Just finish the bathroom," she told him, waving him back to his work. "I'll handle this problem, thank you very much."

"You going to hang your clothes in the garage?" he suggested innocently. That was the only immediate solution to her problem, from what he could see.

"How I resolve my closet issues is my problem," she informed him curtly.

He lingered in the doorway, studying her. "Still mad about yesterday?"

So now he was an analyst, as well? She didn't need anyone shrinking her head for his own amusement. "I'm not 'mad' about yesterday," she retorted.

He was nothing if not flexible. Dealing with third graders did that for a teacher. "Then what are you mad about?"

Her eyes almost blazed as she swung around to face him. "I'm mad that you keep popping up in my life," she told him.

"Oh."

And with that, he went back to the bathroom to continue his work.

She couldn't believe it, but she found herself following him into the semi-gutted master bath. "What, nothing to say? No fancy comeback?" she challenged. "Just 'Oh'?"

He stood there for a moment, as if considering the challenge she'd thrown down. But then he merely shook his head. "I've got nothing," he told her honestly.

"So you've got no argument, no explanation?" she asked incredulously.

If she meant to goad him, her effort fell short of its mark, because he replied in a calm voice, "None I can think of."

"And all this is just one big 'coincidence'?" she asked sarcastically.

His face was totally unreadable. "Looks that way to me."

Her eyebrows drew together in a large, condemning V. "I don't believe you."

He was completely unfazed. "Believe what you want. That is your right under the laws of this great country. I can't make you believe me. But all I know is that I had nothing to do with any of this. I didn't come looking for you, suggesting bathroom renovations, and I had no idea that you taught at Bedford Elementary.

"In each case, all I did was pick up my phone and answer it when it rang. Fate did the rest," Eddie told her, with a whimsical note in his voice.

"Oh, so it was Fate that brought us together," she mocked.

Eddie's shoulders rose in a careless shrug. "It's as good an explanation as any, from where I'm standing."

With that, he picked up the first box of small, pearl-gray tiles and began to fit them together against the wall he had just prepared.

Refusing to drop the subject, Tiffany wanted to hear his explanation. "And why would Fate do something like that?"

"Because," he told her, his mouth curving almost seductively, "apparently she has a wicked sense of humor."

The calmer he sounded, the more infuriated Tiffany felt herself growing. "Then Fate is one seriously deranged entity."

For just a second, he raised his eyes to hers. "Or maybe she knows something we don't," he suggested.

Tiffany squared her shoulders. "Like what?"

He merely smiled at her. "If I knew that, then I wouldn't have used the word *something*, now would I?"

What was there about this man that pressed every single button she had? "I don't know what you would have done. I'm not an expert on you," she reminded him with mounting annoyance. "I don't know anything about you anymore."

"If you don't, then why are you acting as if I'm a walking carrier of the black plague?" Eddie asked her innocently.

She didn't answer him. She couldn't. For the life of her, she didn't know why the very thought of him set her off the way it did.

Oh, she had a dozen little reasons—maybe even a dozen and a half—but if she was being honest with herself, none of them was enough to create these sudden waves of anger she kept experiencing.

But there was always something, right from the beginning, that managed to set her off. And for the life of her, she had no explanation as to why—and even *that* made her crazy.

She was going around in circles, Tiffany thought. And none of this was getting her anywhere. The longer she remained upstairs, supposedly trying to get to the bottom of this constant bickering that was going on between them, the more entrenched she was becoming in all of this.

Which would lead nowhere.

And she didn't know about Montoya, but she had a life to live.

Finding something to put on—not what she was looking for, but it would do—Tiffany grabbed it and a pair of jeans, as well as a change of underwear, and went downstairs.

She'd just finished with her shower and had made her way into the kitchen when her landline rang. Apparently everyone liked getting a jump start on the day, weekend or no weekend, she thought grudgingly as she picked up the receiver.

"Hello?"

"Tiffany, it's Chelsea. The flowers are absolutely beautiful," the voice on the other end of the line told her with effusive enthusiasm.

After her clash with Montoya in the parking lot last night, Tiffany had been moved to call a florist and place an order. She'd had an arrangement of pink roses with a heavy dose of baby's breath sent to Chelsea's home. Not out of any sense of competition for once, but because she felt remiss in not doing something like that on her own before now.

Upon closer examination, not wanting to disturb her friend for a couple weeks had seemed like a paltry excuse.

"They arrived early," Tiffany commented, surprised. She'd thought that the arrangement would go out at noon. "I hope the deliveryman didn't wake you up."

"Oh, that's all right. I only sleep in ten-minute catnaps these days, so they didn't really wake me," the new mother replied with a laugh. And then she changed the direction of the conversation slightly. "Did you know that that new teacher who took over for me brought my whole class to see me?" There was a note of awe and wonder in her voice.

Tiffany pressed her lips together. There was just no getting away from this man in any sense of the word. If she wasn't looking at him, she was hearing about him.

"I heard a rumor," she finally replied.

"He seems like a really nice man," Chelsea went on to say.

"Yes, he does *seem* like that," Tiffany responded, emphasizing the word Chelsea had used.

"So, do you know him? Have you worked with him before?" Chelsea pressed.

It was way too early in the morning for her to get into this now. She hadn't even had her coffee yet.

"We've met," she answered vaguely.

Chelsea apparently didn't pick up on her tone, but said, "I think he's awfully nice, Tiffany. Maybe the two of you could go out for coffee or even for a drink some time."

Oh no, she had to put a stop to this before Chelsea said anything more or got really carried away. "Hey, Miss Cupid, don't you think you have enough on your hands right now without thinking about trying to do any matchmaking?" Tiffany asked.

But it was obvious that Chelsea wasn't about to take the hint. She didn't seem to want to back off. "It's just that I'm so very happy, Tiffany. And when I feel this way, I want to see everyone around me feeling happy, too."

"That's really a wonderful sentiment, Chelsea," Tiffany agreed, doing her best not to sound irritated. "But I don't…"

She was desperately searching for a way to ease out of the conversation, since it was definitely going in a direction she wanted nothing to do with.

But as it turned out, she didn't need to come up with an excuse. Suddenly, there was the distinct sound of wailing in the background.

"Uh-oh, looks like I've got to cut this short, Tiffany," Chelsea apologized. "My daughter is summoning me."

"It sounds like that little girl has got a really great set of lungs," Tiffany commented.

Her friend laughed. "Oh, you don't know the half of it. As soon as she's old enough, Jeff and I are sending her off to opera camp."

Her own humor restored, Tiffany said, "I'll call you later today to find out when's a good time for me to drop by."

"Anytime," Chelsea told her. "Like I said, I'm awake 24/7."

"Just like an all-night pharmacy," Tiffany quipped.

"Exactly."

"I'll still call ahead to let you know when I'm coming," she promised. "Bye."

When Chelsea had bid her goodbye Tiffany hung up the receiver, then turned around to find that she wasn't alone.

Montoya was standing in her kitchen.

Chapter Ten

"Is eavesdropping formally written on your résumé, or are you just developing new skills?" Tiffany asked.

She hadn't heard Eddie Montoya walk in, and even though nothing had been said on the phone that she didn't want overheard, she didn't like being startled this way.

"Neither," he replied, "but you were on the phone and I didn't think it was polite to interrupt you."

Well, that took the wind out of her sails. How did the man always manage to turn things around to make them sound like he was the good guy no matter what the situation? He used to do that when they were back in college, too, she recalled.

Suppressing a sigh, she let the matter of his sudden, unannounced appearance drop, and asked, "What was it you wanted to interrupt me about?"

"Did anyone call you from that porcelain store to give you a revised delivery date for the tub?"

She looked at him as if he wasn't making any sense. "There was no call for a revised delivery date for the tub. It was delivered on Thursday, just as they promised," she told him. "My sister Brittany gave me an earful because she had to sit around most of the day, waiting for the deliverymen to get here. They came pretty late."

In Tiffany's opinion, her sister Brittany had a black belt in complaining. Brittany was usually the last one she turned to when it came to any sort of an involved favor, but all her other sisters were busy that day.

"They delivered it?" Eddie repeated uncertainly. It wasn't in either the bathroom or the bedroom, and it was too big an item to miss if it was anywhere else in the house. "But it's not upstairs."

She already knew that. "That's because they put it in the garage."

The second she said that, Eddie started walking past her to a door just off the kitchen that led into the two-car garage. He opened it and peered in.

She was right; the tub was there. Or at least the heavy-duty cardboard container proclaiming to have a state-of-the-art tub complete with built-in Jacuzzi jets inside it was there.

Eddie frowned as he sighed. The tub didn't do him any good down here.

"Why didn't they carry it upstairs?" he muttered, circling the cardboard container. It seemed to grow bigger with each pass he made around the box.

"Probably because my sister forgot to tell them to take it upstairs." She'd refrained from complaining about the oversight to Brittany because she knew if she did, Brittany would never again do her another favor. Noting the consternation on the contractor's face, Tiffany bit her lower lip. "Is this a bad thing?"

"Not unless you don't mind taking your baths in the garage," he said, annoyed with this latest delay.

Eddie had been hoping to have everything connected by late tonight. Now it looked as if that wasn't going to happen.

Tiffany never even hesitated. "We can get this upstairs."

"We?" He looked at her skeptically. She was five foot four in her bare feet, and although nicely put together, he doubted if she weighed more than about a hundred twenty pounds unless she put rocks in her pockets. That didn't exactly project the picture of strength. "Unless you are really good at levitating heavy objects, I'm going to have to call around and see if I can get someone to come over to give me a hand with this."

"You don't have to call anyone," she insisted. "I'm here."

"I noticed."

When, hands on her hips, she took a determined step forward, he almost laughed out loud, managing to catch himself at the last moment. "No offense, Tiffany, but you don't exactly remind me of a weightlifter."

"No," she agreed, "but I know all about leverage and torque and pulley systems, and that kind of thing beats brute strength every time."

Thinking that he needed to humor her at least to some degree, Eddie said, "I'm listening."

"I've got a couple of furniture dollies in the garage.

We can use them to get the tub out of the garage, up the driveway and into the house."

That sounded reasonable enough, he supposed. But that wasn't the main problem. "And then what?" he asked, expecting her to look flustered.

She didn't. Instead, Tiffany went through her plan for him step by step. As she spoke, Eddie got the distinct impression she had done this before.

"And then we tie the rope around the back of the tub and loop it around the top of the banister. We slant the box with the tub onto the stairs, and then you pull the rope while I push the tub up from the rear."

He frowned. Was she kidding? "You can't push the tub up the stairs."

She answered him in all seriousness. "Well, it's easier than pulling the rope, even with torque, but I'll do that if you want to be the one to push." She saw the expression on his face, as if he was wondering if she'd gone over the edge. "Don't look at me like that. This system worked when I used it to get the bureau into my bedroom, and I was alone when I did that."

He was still staring at her as if she was spinning tall tales, and she was coming to the end of her patience. "What?" she demanded.

Eddie had gone over what she'd just told him, and after being highly skeptical, he began to think that maybe, just maybe, there was a chance of making this work without calling in favors from friends he'd help move.

He had to admit that she'd surprised him. "You came up with this idea on your own?"

She shoved her hands into her back pockets to keep from shrugging her shoulders in a self-deprecating way.

"Beats making a pest out of myself and asking for help all the time. FYI, not every deliveryman is willing to bring things up to the second floor. Any other questions?" she asked, waiting to hear his objections—and then shoot them down.

"Yeah." He looked around the garage. "Where's the rope?"

She knew exactly where the coils of rope were, could lay her hands on them within a couple minutes and told him so. When she saw that he was watching her with that incredulous expression again, she could tell exactly what he was thinking this time.

"It's an organization thing," she told him. "I learned it in self-defense. There were five of us in two bedrooms when I was a kid and none of us could leave our rooms, even to go to school, unless everything there was neatly put away—in its proper place, according to my mother."

Since Tiffany had indicated that she had a rope, they needed only one other thing to get started. "And the dollies?"

"Right here," she announced, marching across the garage. She took both dollies from their place against the far wall, wheeled them over and placed them next to the cardboard container.

Eddie seemed to contemplate which end of the tub to lift first so that he could slide one of the dollies under it.

"Hold it," she suddenly cried.

He slanted a look at her. "Nothing to hold yet," he pointed out. "Something wrong?"

"No, I just forgot a step," she confessed, going over to one of the metal shelves on the side of the garage.

"I think it's best if we secure the tub onto the dollies with bungee cords. That way it stands less of a chance of falling off."

He laughed, shaking his head as she returned with an entire collection of bungee cords in different sizes. "Who are you, MacGyver?"

She wasn't sure what he was talking about. "Just someone who believes in being prepared."

Lifting one end of the boxed tub, Eddie was about to try to maneuver one of the dollies under it with his foot when Tiffany quickly pushed the device into position. Then, moving fast, she secured it with a wide bungee cord.

In short order, the process was repeated with the other end of the tub.

"I've got to say that you are the most unique woman I have ever known," Eddie marveled.

She regarded him doubtfully for a moment. "I'm not sure if that's a compliment."

"Well, let me assure you I meant it as one," he told her.

Tiffany nodded, but she still wasn't certain how to react to his comment. She knew what to do and say when she was up against insults or criticisms, but not when it came to an actual personal compliment, Especially coming from him.

It was one thing for her to receive praise and accolades at school or in some sort of an assembly situation. She could handle that. But to hear a compliment from a slightly sweaty, sexy-looking male standing in close proximity to her in her garage was a whole different story.

It was almost *too* private—and that was an area

she had promised herself never to revisit, especially with the likes of Montoya.

Telling herself to move on, she said, "Okay then, let's get this thing out of the garage and into the house."

He glanced at the container and dollies. "Do you want me in the front or in the back?"

Where had that sudden wave of blanketing heat come from? She could feel a line of perspiration forming along the top of her forehead, just beneath her hairline.

Tiffany cleared her throat, hoping her voice wouldn't suddenly crack. "The front. Guide it from the front. I'll bring up the rear—I mean the back…" That still didn't sound right. "Whatever," she finally said in desperation. "Let's just go."

Working together and moving rather slowly, they maneuvered the boxed tub up the single step from the front of the house into the foyer, then to the foot of the stairs.

"Okay, time for part two," she said, going back into the garage to get the coiled rope.

Eddie was expecting ordinary, run-of-the-mill rope and was surprised when she brought back two large balls of coarse, thick hemp.

"You actually had these in your garage?" he marveled, looking over one of the balls. Obviously there was a side to this woman he never knew existed.

She didn't understand why Eddie sounded so surprised. It was just rope. Granted, it was rather coarse, but that also made it stronger. "Yes, why?"

He laughed softly to himself. "Like I said, you are really unique."

"Oh, I forgot to mention one important part," Tiffany recalled, as she began to secure the rope carefully around the box.

"Bringing in two six-foot-six, burly movers?" Eddie suggested.

"No." Running up the stairs with the rope, she passed it around the top banister post, then took the end with her into the bedroom. He followed her to see what she was up to. "I forgot to mention securing the rope around the leg of the bed frame. It helps supply better torque."

He watched as she wiggled under the bed, then carefully made her way back out. He knew he shouldn't have stared at the way her butt moved as she did that, but he was only human—and feeling more so as he went on observing her shapeliness.

"And you really came up with this by yourself?" he asked when she was done.

He'd already asked that once. Tiffany was immediately on the defensive. "Why? Are you going to make fun of me because I did?"

"No," he declared. "I'm going to tell you that I'm really impressed. I wouldn't have thought of anything like that."

A warmth moved up her neck, and she struggled to ignore it. The last thing she wanted was for color to creep up into her cheeks. "Yeah, well, you know the old saying about necessity being the mother of invention. You'd be surprised with what you can come up with when you have to. Here." She handed him the rope. "You pull and I'll push."

"Wait," he called after her as she raced down the stairs.

She swung around on the last step. "What?" she asked impatiently.

"We need to angle the box onto the stairs first, remember?" He made his way down to the landing. "As good as you are, I don't think you can do that on your own."

Was he being sarcastic? Tiffany wondered. But when she looked at his face, ready to challenge him, he didn't seem to be mocking her.

"Okay, let's do it," she agreed.

Between them, they managed to angle the large container onto the stairs just enough to be able to execute the rest of Tiffany's elaborately simple system—as soon as Eddie got back up to the top.

"Do you have enough room to get by?" Tiffany asked, concerned when she saw that the gap left between the wall and the box seemed exceedingly slim.

Eddie eyed the space. "I guess I'll have to," he said philosophically.

Pressing himself as flat as he could against the wall, he managed to squeeze past the box. Moments later he was at the top of the stairs, in position. "Okay, I've got the rope," he announced.

"Pull!" she ordered as she began to push against the bottom of the container with all her might, using her left shoulder as well as her hands.

While tugging the rope toward him, Eddie couldn't help but be in awe of Tiffany's ingenuity. What she had managed to rig up was a glorified pulley system, and thanks to the fact that she was apparently far stronger than she looked, the operation worked beautifully. Slowly, perhaps, but effectively.

After a great deal of pulling and pushing, and more

than an abundance of sweating, the tub, still securely packed in its container, finally made it to the second floor.

As did the two of them.

Once the tub was flat on the landing and a foot toward the bedroom, Tiffany came up the last two steps behind it and literally collapsed on the floor, lying on her back.

"We…did it…" she gasped. She was so exhausted she was afraid she would have stopped breathing if she'd fallen face forward on the carpeting.

Eddie saw no reason to play the mighty macho male, and collapsed to the floor on the other side of the tub. All he saw of Tiffany was her feet.

"You…did it…" he corrected, his voice as breathless as hers. "It was…your…idea," he panted.

She wanted to raise her head to look at him. As it turned out, all she could do was turn it in his direction. She addressed her words to the container. "Why are you being so nice?" she asked, suspicious.

His breathing was slowing getting under control. "I believe in giving credit where credit's due. Besides, I was never *not* nice," he protested with a complete lack of energy.

"Yes…you were," she contradicted, pausing between each word. "Not nice, I mean. You were always competitive, always trying to beat me, to outdo me."

Eddie frowned. She was remembering something that really wasn't true. Oh, there was no denying that, a time or two, he'd set out to do better than she did, but she was his yardstick. He measured his own accomplishments against hers. She was the one he had to be as good as, or better than, if he wanted to be a good teacher.

"No, I wasn't," he protested. But there was no way he was about to get into that argument. "That's all in your head." And then, snaking forward a couple inches so he could see her, he turned his head in her direction and offered an exhausted smile. "Another way of saying it is that I brought out the best in you, that's all."

Which just meant that he thought he was better than she was. "No, I—"

"I'm really exhausted, Tiffany," he told her, raising his voice and cutting into whatever she was about to say. "Okay if I just lie here for a little while longer?"

"Sure. Go ahead. Maybe I'll even join you," she said, not focusing on the fact that she hadn't gotten up yet and was still lying there herself.

"Sounds like a plan to me," he mumbled.

For the next few minutes, there was nothing but the sound of their rather uneven breathing. It was the most peaceful few minutes they'd known yet.

Chapter Eleven

When she heard Montoya calling to her from the master bath, Tiffany braced herself. It was almost seven in the evening, and judging from the noises she'd heard over the last eleven hours, Eddie had been at work on the bathroom renovations the entire time.

Even so, given the hour, what she was bracing herself to hear was that he was going to have to come back tomorrow morning because the job still wasn't finished.

Which meant, she thought gloomily, that once again she wouldn't be sleeping in. Still, she supposed she couldn't really be upset about that, considering the fact that Eddie *was* working hard.

Abandoning the paperwork she'd been engrossed in, and which she had spread out all over the sectional sofa—neatness was not something she was fanatical about when it came to her own life—Tiffany went upstairs.

"Look, it's all right if you're not finished," she began, before she took one step into the bathroom.

"Who says I'm not finished?" Eddie asked as he rose to his feet.

All over his shirtless torso his skin had a fine sheen, comprised of his own sweat mingled with dust, dirt and what looked to be splotches of glue he'd been using. He turned around to face her.

What she was most aware of was not the sweat, but the sculpted muscles that seemed to get bigger every time she saw them. She was also aware of his wall-to-wall smile. Filled with dazzling white teeth, it was the kind of pleased, triumphant grin that could have easily belonged to the top-ranking champion of the playground wars as he happily announced, "There, I told you I could do it!"

Eddie didn't say any such words, but they were clearly implied as well as embedded in his smile as he turned it, full blast, in her direction.

His eyes on hers, he swept his hand around her brand-new, completed bathroom. The tile floor looked exactly like gray wood, the same shade as the marble in her shower and her quartz counter. "So, what do you think?"

She honestly hadn't expected it to be finished yet. After she'd seen the bathroom gutted last Saturday, the full extent of the work that needed to be done had finally hit her. At this point, she'd thought it would take him not just one more day, but at least a week, if not more. The fact that he was done stunned her.

"I think you must have had elves helping you,"

she told him, amazed at the difference between the incomplete bathroom she'd had a week ago and what she was looking at now.

"Couldn't reach them," he told her with a deadly serious face. "They're on vacation and the cell phone reception there is murder. Besides, they've gone union on me."

His humor went right over her head. She hardly heard him. Like someone in one of those home makeover programs, Tiffany slowly moved passed him with small steps, as if in a trance. Her eyes were huge as she looked around.

Everything was beautiful! And perfect.

"You *did* all this?" There was unabashed wonder in her voice.

Eddie had learned a long time ago to hedge his bets and to be cautious. "Let me ask you a question first—do you like it?"

"Yes, oh yes," she cried, spinning around the newly remodeled bathroom. "This is better than I ever thought possible."

"Then yes, I did all this," he answered, pleased with her reaction and rather pleased with his own work. He was his own hardest taskmaster, but he also knew when to step back and bask in his accomplishments.

The thought hit Tiffany belatedly. She turned to look at him for a second. "And if I didn't like it?" she asked, wanting to see what he'd say.

"Then I'd still say yes, but I'd say it closer to the top of the stairs"

She didn't understand what he was telling her. "Why the stairs?"

"That way, I'd have a running start," he told her with a short laugh. "In case you wanted to pound on me for messing up your bathroom."

She offered a careless shrug in response. "I would've have caught up to you anyway."

"Oh, I have my doubts."

The words had just slipped out. He hadn't meant to taunt her. He knew what she was like when it came to any sort of a competition, real or imagined. She absolutely refused to be bested.

Eddie immediately jumped in in an attempt to deflect whatever was coming. "Well, I'm starving, so if you don't mind, I'm going to pack up my tools and go get something to eat."

Tiffany realized that he'd literally been slaving here all day. Other contractors would have dragged the process out by at least another day, if not two. Instead, he'd worked straight through in order to finish the job for her.

The least she could do was to feed the man.

The problem was, she wasn't one of those people who could look inside an almost empty refrigerator and, using a little of this, a little of that, throw together an outstanding meal. She was more like one of those people who looked into a refrigerator that was filled to the brim and scratched her head, not having a clue what to serve.

There was only one thing she could actually safely cook. Tiffany fell back on that now as she offered to prepare it for him.

"I could scramble up some eggs and serve it with toast for you," she told him.

Eddie looked at her, confusion in his eyes. And then he glanced at his watch.

"Is something wrong?" Tiffany asked.

"No." He dropped his hand to his side. "I thought that maybe I'd worked straight through the night without realizing it." Then, because her puzzled expression seemed to only intensify, he explained why he'd said that. "You just offered to make me breakfast."

"That's because scrambled eggs and toast are the only things I actually know I can make." Saying that, Tiffany was immediately braced for a fight. "And if you make fun of that, so help me…"

It was his turn to look puzzled. "Why should I make fun of that?" he asked her. "I happen to love scrambled eggs."

Her eyebrows drew together in a squiggle as she tried to assess whether or not Eddie was being sarcastic. "Seriously?"

"Why would I bother lying about something like that?" he asked her.

Maybe she was being too defensive, Tiffany told herself. Besides, the man had worked hard all day. She needed to set aside her combative nature, at least for a little while.

"Okay," she declared, "then scrambled eggs and toast it is. Give me a few minutes to get started, then come down," she told him. With that, she began to quickly walk out of the master bathroom.

"Why don't you make that for two?" Eddie called after her.

Surprised, Tiffany paused just outside the doorway. Feeling guilty that he had gone this long without stopping to get something to eat, she tried to cover up her remiss behavior by asking the first thing that came to mind. "Are you that hungry?"

"No, I just don't like eating alone—if I can help it," he added.

Tiffany looked at him in silence for a long moment. And then she nodded. "All right, two it is," she told him, turning away.

The next moment, she was hurrying down the stairs.

"You did a really nice job," she stated, once she had put out the two plates and had seated herself at the table opposite him.

Eddie smiled at the compliment, knowing that it couldn't have been easy for her to say anything positive to him. In most of their encounters over the years, it had been the exact opposite. For the life of him, he didn't understand this rivalry she seemed to think existed between them, but he supposed that his reaction to her attitude probably had at least a little something to do with the rivalry continuing.

"So did you," he told her, easily returning the compliment.

The confusion was back in her eyes as she shook her head. "I don't understand. I didn't do anything."

"Yes, you did," he contradicted. Indicating the dishes before them, he said, "You made scrambled eggs and toast."

Her confusion gave way to anger. She was back on the defensive. "Now you *are* making fun of me," Tiffany accused.

"No, I'm not," he insisted. He didn't want to start something at this late hour of the day. Tired, he was afraid he might say something he'd regret. But even so, he felt he had to at least *try* to make her understand what he'd meant. "You said you didn't cook, but this is great, and I just thought I should tell you."

Tiffany still wasn't completely certain that he wasn't mocking her. "They're just eggs," she said dismissively.

"But they can still be messed up," he pointed out. He paused to consume the last bite on his plate. "I know people who can literally burn water."

"How do you burn water?" she challenged.

"That's simple," he responded, vividly remembering an incident. "You boil it until it evaporates and winds up burning the bottom of the pot."

He sounded as if he'd experienced that firsthand. "Girlfriend?" Tiffany asked, before she could stop herself.

She didn't want him thinking that she was curious about his private life. She couldn't care less about it. Or so she silently tried to convince herself.

"Older sister," Eddie corrected. "Elena. She was really awful. My mother was horrified when she realized that Ellie couldn't cook to save her life, and she immediately took her in hand."

Tiffany was only half listening. Her mind was racing around, trying to negate her error. "I shouldn't have asked," she told him.

He clearly didn't understand. "Why not?"

"Because your personal life is none of my business," she said dismissively.

He laughed. "There's nothing 'personal' about my sisters, trust me," Eddie assured her. "With all the different forms of social media available to them, my sisters wind up posting every little detail about their lives. I love them, but they're just way too open and out there for me," he confessed.

"I meant *your* life," Tiffany said, still trying to gracefully backtrack out of what she felt was an obvious error on her part.

Eddie watched her, a look of curiosity in his eyes, behind his genial expression. She was beginning to regret offering to feed him. Things were getting too complicated.

"What about my life?" he asked.

Was he tangling up her words on purpose, or was she the one at fault, tripping on her own tongue and talking gibberish? She wasn't sure.

"Nothing," she answered rather adamantly. The next moment, she was standing up, holding her empty plate and getting ready to deposit it in the sink. "You're probably exhausted. Why don't you go home?"

She'd tried to sound as tactful as possible, but it was obvious she'd failed when she heard Eddie start to laugh.

"What's your hurry—here's your hat," he said, quoting an old joke to indicate that he knew she was all but physically ushering him out of the house. Getting up from the table, he nodded at his empty dish. "Thanks for the eggs and toast. I'll just go get my stuff and I'll be out of your hair before you know it."

Tiffany felt she should be polite and protest that he wasn't "in her hair," but they both knew his presence here was unsettling to her. Granted, they were getting along, at least for the moment, but there was no denying the fact that there was this agitated feeling in the pit of her stomach just being around him.

She couldn't explain why that was. Things had changed since college. It wasn't as if they were competing with one another—or that Montoya was somehow trying to show her up in some way or other. If anything, he was being nice—and yet she couldn't shake that image that was running though her mind. The image that her sister had mentioned and likened her to the other week. That of a cat on a hot tin roof.

She actually did feel like a cat on a hot tin roof, unable to maintain its balance because the roof was burning its paws.

But why did Eddie Montoya make her feel that way? What was there about this man that threw her into confusion like this?

Stop overthinking it. Some things just are, Tiffany silently insisted.

Lost in thought, she didn't realize that Eddie had come down from upstairs, his toolbox in one hand, until he was standing right beside her.

"I'll see you on Monday," he told her as he walked past.

"Right, Monday. Eddie," she said suddenly, just as he reached for the front door.

He paused and looked at her over his shoulder, the expression on his face saying that he was braced to hear her cite some oversight on his part. It was obvious he had come to expect that from her.

"I don't know if I made myself clear earlier, but you really did do a very nice job on my bathroom," Tiffany forced herself to tell him. Only steely self-control kept her from shifting from one foot to the other like some insecure, errant child. She *hated* that he had this effect on her.

She was rewarded with the same wide grin she'd seen when he'd called her into the bathroom earlier. She felt her stomach tighten in response. But instead of thanking her the way she expected him to, he told her, "You did—kind of."

And with that, he closed the door behind him. Leaving her staring at it, an odd mixture of annoyance and—was that longing?—churning through her veins.

She wanted to throw open the door and yell something at him, a retort to put him in his place—but she couldn't think of anything to say.

And besides, he hadn't actually said anything bad. He'd said exactly what she'd all but said to him. That she hadn't really made it clear that he'd done a good job with this remodeling.

She was bright enough to know that there were two ways a bathroom renovation could go. The way it had for her, and the way that nightmares were made of. The latter usually turned out to be very costly and time consuming, especially when it came to undoing the damage a bad contractor left in his wake and redoing the job properly. Montoya had definitely spared her having to go through all that.

So why did she have this fierce desire to pummel him to the ground with her fists? Where was all this residual hostility coming from and how did she pack it away properly so that it wouldn't get in her way? She was going to have to deal with him on a regular basis. He was a teacher in her school, at least until the end of the school year. That meant she needed to get a grip.

Now.

* * *

Tiffany slept in the next day. *Way* in. But even the extra hours of sleep—she woke up at noon—didn't seem to help her find the peace of mind she needed. Nor did it help her untangle the heavily knotted skein of feelings that only seemed to be growing in size within her.

When the landline beside her bed rang, she lunged for it.

"Hello?" It was half a greeting, half a demand.

"You can't still be asleep, can you?" the male voice asked.

Instantly alert, she scrambled into a sitting position and leaned back against her headboard. "I'm awake," she lied. "Why are you calling?"

"I think I left one of my tools in your bathroom last night."

"And you want to come over to look for it," she guessed. Talk about a flimsy excuse to drop in. She would have expected him to be more creative than that.

She didn't realize she was smiling until she caught sight of herself in the mirror over the bureau.

"No," Eddie said, surprising her. "I just wanted you to bring it to school tomorrow, in case you happen to find it," he told her.

"Sure, I can do that," she told him.

He described the tool, a specialized hammer. "Okay," he concluded. "Thanks."

The next minute the connection between them had terminated.

Tiffany sat there for a moment, looking at the receiver. And then she sighed and returned it to the cradle.

She felt oddly disappointed as she got up to take her shower—and told herself she was crazy.

Chapter Twelve

Tiffany stifled a yawn as she walked into school the next morning. This getting up earlier than she had to was becoming a habit, one she wasn't thrilled about. But she wanted to get to Eddie's classroom and leave that hammer he'd called about before he turned up this morning. She was back to trying to avoid interacting with him as much as possible—until she at least had a chance to shut down these stray thoughts that kept popping up in her head.

Last night she'd dreamed about Eddie, not once but three separate times. Each time, she awoke with a jolt, unable to pin down what her dream was about, only that it had included Eddie and that she'd woken up feeling warm all over.

She didn't want him invading her thoughts, consciously or unconsciously, and certainly not her dreams. The only way she could see to keep him from doing that, other than to change schools, was to limit her interaction with the man as much as possible. Now that he was no longer remodeling her bathroom, that seemed rather doable.

Planning on leaving the hammer in the middle drawer of his desk—leaving it in plain sight might prove to be too tempting to any student who might come in early—Tiffany had gotten as far as crossing the room when she heard that unmistakable deep voice ask, "Can I help you with something?"

Startled, she got ahold of herself before she turned around. The process involved talking herself out of having goose bumps.

There was the tall, dark and just-too-handsome-for-her-own-good teacher standing less than a foot away.

How had he managed to sneak up on her like that without making any noise? It didn't seem possible. It wasn't as if he was some ninety-pound weakling. His muscular frame undoubtedly weighed more than that, she thought grudgingly.

"I was just going to put this in the middle drawer of your desk," she explained.

He didn't want her opening that drawer, not until he was ready to show her what he had in there.

"That's all right. I'll take it." Eddie put his hand out, and with a shrug, she gave him the hammer. "Thanks for bringing it in."

Rather than putting it in the middle drawer, he tucked it away in one of the desk's side drawers.

"Sure, no problem." This was where she left the room, Tiffany told herself. But for some reason, she remained. And even told him something she knew she shouldn't. "You know, when you called, I thought you were using the hammer as an excuse to come back to the house."

Rather than deny the suggestion, or laugh it off the way she expected, he looked into her eyes and quietly asked, "Would I need an excuse to come back to the house? I couldn't just ask to drop by?"

She'd left herself wide open for that one, Tiffany admonished, at a loss as to how to answer his question. Knowing him, he'd wind up challenging her, and she didn't want to be in that position.

"I, um…" Just then, the bell rang, signaling the beginning of the day. She looked upward, as if she'd just been on the receiving end of merciful divine intervention. "There's the morning bell. I'd better get to my classroom," she said, heading for the door without a backward glance.

"Thanks again for bringing the hammer," he called after her.

She could have sworn she heard him softly laughing under his breath, but she would have had to turn around to verify that, and she wanted to avoid any more eye contact with Eddie at all cost. It was ridiculous, but it felt as if he could see right into her head and knew exactly what she was thinking.

That wasn't possible, and yet…

For the umpteenth time, she made up her mind to avoid *any* contact with the man. And it should be possible, she silently argued. After all, they taught different grades, and as far as she knew, there were no general staff meetings scheduled in the near future.

Piece of cake, she promised herself.

* * *

It wasn't long before the cake began to crumble.

She'd completely forgotten about the annual relay races for charity that each elementary school in Bedford held in the spring.

The idea was for the students in each class to enlist sponsors to either donate a lump sum to the chosen charity, or pay some specified amount for each lap that the student managed to run. The class that raised the most money won a prize. Meanwhile, the money raised was donated to the local homeless family shelter.

It was a healthy activity, held outdoors, and the students learned what it meant to do something to help those less fortunate than themselves.

It also involved the friendly spirit of competition, since the classes were essentially pitted against one another.

Which in turn meant that her class would be competing against the students in Montoya's class. Not directly, since all the classes were competing with one another in general, but to her, his was the only class that mattered.

Which was why, the moment she remembered about the upcoming race, Tiffany immediately began giving her own students pep talks about "going all out" for the good of the goal.

"You mean beating all the other classes," Danny, one of the boys in her class, said after she had finished giving what she'd felt was a pretty rousing opening speech.

She didn't want it to come across as cold as the boy

made it sound, so she did her best to shine a proper light on the upcoming activity.

"Well, yes, but beating them means that you're the class that ran the most laps and raised the most amount of money for the homeless shelter. That's the bottom line," she stressed.

"I thought the bottom line was winning the prize," another student said, speaking up.

"What is the prize?" Rita asked, raising her voice above the others.

"We get the day off from school to go on a picnic to William Mason Park," Tiffany told her class, mentioning a popular recreation area located in the northern part of the city. Being students, she thought they'd find a sanctioned day *away* from school particularly tempting.

And they did, judging by the chorus of cheers that erupted.

"Sounds good to me," Danny declared approvingly.

"But the main prize..." Tiffany stressed, raising her voice in order to cut through the chatter.

"You mean there's more?" Danny asked.

She'd ascertained that this year, Danny was pretty much her class clown, and for now, she ignored him. "The main prize," she repeated, "is knowing that you've done something good for someone else. Right?" she asked, looking around at the twenty-eight faces before her. When they didn't answer, she repeated, "Right?"

"Yeah, I guess so," Carter, one of the quieter students, mumbled.

"You better believe it," Tiffany told him with an

enthusiasm that quickly spread throughout her entire classroom.

The trouble was, she was forgetting to believe that part herself. At least believe in it as much as she should. Instead, she was getting caught up in this competition *as* a competition, and as a result was forgetting about the good that was being accomplished with this race.

She took herself to task for that. All these years later, and competition was *still* the first thought that entered her head whenever she thought of anything that had to do with Eddie Montoya.

That needed to change. And it would—just as soon as her class won this race.

"Okay, now go out there this afternoon and ring some doorbells," she encouraged, passing out the sign-up pledge sheets. "When this is all over, I want *our* class to be the one that raises the most money to donate to that shelter," she told her students, just before she dismissed them for the day.

They poured out of the room, the sign-up sheets clutched in their hands.

Her little minions, she thought fondly.

"Ever think of becoming a motivational speaker?" Alisha asked her, poking her head into the newly emptied classroom.

"You were eavesdropping?" Tiffany asked, about to gather together her things so she could leave for the day, as well.

"I just stopped by to see you and I couldn't help overhearing. I sent my kids home a couple of minutes early so they could get a head start ringing doorbells," Alisha explained. "But I just told them to do the best that they could. I didn't give them a 'win this one for the Gipper' speech."

Tiffany shrugged. "Neither did I."

"Yeah, right." Alisha laughed. "Tell me, just why is winning this little competition so important to you?" she inquired.

Tiffany zipped up her briefcase. "Winning should be important to everyone, or why bother showing up?" she countered.

Alisha nodded thoughtfully, then smiled knowingly, as if she saw right through what her friend had just said. "You're being evasive." She looked at Tiffany closely. "This wouldn't have anything to do with Tall, Dark and Gorgeous, would it?"

Tiffany frowned. She didn't like being pinned down. "I have no idea what you're talking about."

"Yeah, you do, but I've got a doctor's appointment, so I've got to get out of here. Otherwise, I'd keep after you until I got you to own up," Alisha told her with a laugh.

"A doctor's appointment?" Tiffany repeated. It wasn't like Alisha to just run off to the doctor without a reason. She looked at her friend, concerned. "It's not anything serious, is it?"

Alisha looked as if she was thinking the question over. "I don't know. How serious do you consider having another baby?"

Caught off guard, Tiffany found herself almost stuttering. "Wait—what?"

"Baby. Pregnant," Alisha enunciated, then continued to spell it out slowly, obviously enjoying herself. "I'm in the family way. With child."

"I got it, I got it," Tiffany protested.

"Good," Alisha said, "because I was running out cute phrases for this condition."

Tiffany looked at her friend with a touch of awe as the words continued to sink in. "You're pregnant?"

"That's the general gist of it, yes." The next moment, she found herself caught up in an almost fierce hug as Tiffany enthusiastically embraced her.

"That's wonderful," Tiffany cried. Opening her arms and stepping back, she looked at Alisha, seeing her in this new light. "So, how do you feel?"

"Better now that you've released me. You have some death grip there, Tiffany," she stated. "Save it for Mr. Gorgeous."

A hint of a frown flickered across Tiffany's lips, then receded. "I'm so happy for you, I'll pretend you didn't say that."

"Pretend all you want," Alisha said as she began to leave the room. "But I see chemistry between you and that hunk of a man." She winked as she stressed, "Lots of chemistry."

"While you're at the gynecologist, ask for a referral for a good eye doctor," Tiffany called after her friend. "You definitely need one."

Alisha merely waved her hand over her head, making no verbal acknowledgment.

Tiffany picked up her briefcase and slipped her purse strap onto her shoulder. A bittersweet feeling wafted through her.

A baby, she thought. This would be Alisha's second one. Tiffany felt both elated for Alisha and just the slightest bit jealous, as well, because she would have *loved* to have a baby.

Not much chance of that happening unless You've got plans on the books for another Immaculate Conception, she thought, glancing heavenward.

The next minute, Tiffany remembered that she had someplace to be herself. Her oldest sister's house. She'd promised Brittany that she would babysit the twins so that her sister and brother-in-law could have a much needed evening out. It was her way of repaying Brittany for spending all day Thursday waiting for the tub to be delivered.

For now, Alisha, babies and competitive races were placed on the back burner.

Tiffany spent the rest of the week encouraging her students to collect as many pledges as they could without causing a revolt in their neighborhoods. She even located photographs on the internet chronicling the way the homeless shelter had initially looked when it opened, and how it looked now.

The building, thanks to the generosity of others, had practically doubled in size. She made a point of telling her students that while the facility had grown, unfortunately, the number of people who found themselves in circumstances that made it necessary to avail themselves of the shelter had nearly tripled.

"That means that more cots are needed, more food, more everything," Tiffany told her students, slipping the photographs back into the folder she'd brought to class.

"More everything?" Jonathan Keen, one of the more vocal students, questioned. "Like what?"

"Like programs to help reeducate a lot of the

homeless single mothers who come there. This way, they can eventually provide for themselves and their kids. The shelter doesn't just feed them, it finds ways to help them stand up on their own two feet so they can feed themselves," Tiffany stressed.

"And all that can happen 'cause we're running around in a big circle?" Shelley Martinez asked just a little skeptically.

She liked the fact that her students questioned things. It meant that they were thinking.

"It's a start," she told Shelley. "Never underestimate what you can do to help someone else," Tiffany said, slowly looking at each and every one of them.

The solemn expressions she saw told her that at least some of her students were taking this to heart.

Each day, she felt that her class grew a little more enthusiastic about the fund-raising process. So much so that she began to see her students competing against one another as to who could secure the most pledges. By the time the day of the race arrived two weeks later, it was as if her students were chomping at the bit, more than ready to outrun all the other classes.

With her class gathered around her, Tiffany made a few more adjustments on the sheets she had to hand in to the principal. Two more students had come in with last-minute pledges to add to their tally. Every single student in her class had come through with at least five pledges, if not more. The effort they had put into this was stunning, she thought proudly. Now all they had to do was win the race, so that they could be rewarded.

Students from all the classes gathered in the field directly behind the school. After hours, and on weekends, the field was used for Little League games. And it was the perfect size for a competition of this nature.

The principal slowly made the rounds and reviewed each class's pledge sheets, skimming them quickly. When she came to Tiffany's, the woman appeared exceedingly impressed.

Raising her eyes, she asked, "Is this accurate?"

"Absolutely," Tiffany told her. She noticed Eddie looking in her direction and it was all she could do to keep from grinning from ear to ear. *Gotcha,* she thought. "I just went over it myself this morning."

The principal handed back the pledge sheets. "If these kids do even reasonably well, that shelter is going to be able to build on a new wing," she marveled.

The woman turned toward the field filled with eager faces. In addition, each of the classes had two volunteer parents who were to keep tally of the number of laps completed. "All right, everyone knows the rules," the principal declared. "Run laps for as long as you're comfortable. I don't want anyone overdoing it or getting sick, do you understand?"

"Yes, Mrs. Walters," the students answered in a singsong chorus.

"All right. Mr. Montoya—" Ada Walters turned toward the lone male teacher "—since you're new here, you may do the honors and start this race."

"I'd be happy to." Stepping into the center of the circle, he took a long look around at the eager participants of the first four classes that were running.

"All right, everyone, get on your mark. Get set. Go!" he declared.

A volley of cheers erupted, accompanying the sound of pounding sneakers hitting the asphalt track.

Eddie quickly stepped back into the outer circle, comprised of teachers and parents.

Tiffany realized that somehow he had managed to turn up beside her. Was that on purpose, or wasn't he paying attention?

"Shouldn't you be with the other third-grade teacher?" she asked.

He gave her a disarming smile that, try as she might, she couldn't seem to build up an immunity to. "I didn't realize there was a caste system in effect at the school."

"There isn't. I just thought that you'd feel more comfortable next to the teachers from the other lower grades," Tiffany replied.

"No, not particularly," he told her. "Besides, I think that your students are as pumped up as mine are, so maybe this might be the right place for me to be, after all."

She was not going to let him erode the confidence she was experiencing in her students. "Is that your way of saying that you think your students could actually stand a chance of coming in close to mine?"

"That's my way of saying that I think my students might even *beat* your students," he replied honestly.

She raised her chin. "How would you like to make a small wager on that?"

"I'd hate to take your money."

Was he being condescending? She felt her temper rising. "But I won't hate to take yours," she countered.

"Ten dollars says my class beats yours." Putting her hand out, she asked, "Bet?"

"Bet," he said with a grin, his hand all but swallowing hers up.

Chapter Thirteen

Looking back after the fact, it was beyond a doubt the most exhausting fifty-five minutes Tiffany recalled ever having spent. Fifty-five minutes that came after what felt like an endurance test of over three hours.

Because there were six grades and two classes of each, the races were conducted using only two grades at a time, or four classes in total.

Technically, Eddie's third graders did not compete against her fifth graders, but Tiffany was very aware of the total number of laps his class ran. Competitive though she was, Eddie's class's numbers were the only ones that actually mattered to her.

While the other classes all did fairly well, the students in them acted more like they were involved in an event than a competition. Once their part in the race was over, they were just glad to collapse on the grass and sip the fruit drinks that had been provided by the volunteer parents, as well as the teachers.

But unlike the other classes, Eddie's students, she observed, ran as if they were all competing for gold medals in some sort of Junior Olympics. They didn't just run, they fairly *flew* around the large, newly re-painted oval track.

And then it was her class's turn.

"It looks like Mr. Montoya's class is the one to beat if you want to win that picnic in the park," Tiffany told her students as they huddled around her.

Because of the intense way she felt, there was more that Tiffany wanted to say, but she knew she couldn't, in all good conscience, transfer her own desire to best Eddie onto her fifth graders. If nothing else, that would be putting too much pressure on them.

So, reining herself in, Tiffany concluded her pep talk by saying, "Do the best you can. Nobody can ask more of you than that."

"Run with us, Ms. Lee," Danny suddenly urged.

A few of the other students spoke up, backing up Danny's enthusiastic request. "C'mon, it'll make us run faster."

Tiffany sincerely doubted that, but she knew she couldn't very well decline, especially when some of the other teachers had joined their classes for a lap. A couple had even done two. She couldn't turn her class down.

"Yeah, Mr. Montoya ran with his class and they're just babies," Anita piped.

Like the other teachers, Tiffany had dressed casu-ally today. She was wearing sneakers and jeans, so she had no excuse to fall back on. The fact that she wasn't one of those people who found running exhilarating didn't really help her in this instance.

"Okay, I'll run," she reluctantly agreed. "But you can't make fun of me when this is all over."

"We wouldn't make fun of you, Ms. Lee," one of her students promised.

"Lending moral support?" Eddie asked her as he once again walked into the center of the oval. The principal had him starting each of the races.

"You ran with your class," Tiffany pointed out, secretly praying she wasn't going to be making a fool of herself.

"So now you have to run with yours," he said. It wasn't a question, but a conclusion on his part.

Before she had a chance to respond, Eddie did the standard countdown and then shouted, "Go!"

The last four grades were off and running.

At first, Tiffany was uncomfortably aware that her "nemesis" was watching her. Worried about falling down right in front of him, it was all she could do to keep running and not trip over her own feet—or over a student.

The first lap seemed to take forever. The second only a fraction less time.

And then a strange thing happened.

Even though she had promised herself to stop at the end of the next lap, she didn't. Silently challenging herself, Tiffany just kept going. One lap fed into another and then another.

Little by little, the cluster of runners moving around the oval began to thin out.

Forty runners became twenty and then twenty became ten. Ten became less in a sporadic pattern, until there were only three runners left—two of her students and Tiffany herself.

She wasn't sure just how much longer any of them could have lasted, but that was the point when, mercifully, the principal blew her whistle.

As Tiffany heard herself panting, Mrs. Walters walked into the center of the painted circle, held up her hand and announced, "I officially declare this year's Race for the Shelter to be over! Stop running, you three, you're making the rest of us exhausted."

Students, teachers and parents all laughed. Tiffany and her two students were far too tired to join in. The principal's voice seemed to drone on as she told the rest of the school how well they had done.

Tiffany's legs felt as if they had somehow transformed into soggy cotton. They were so wobbly that she was actually afraid to attempt to walk back to her classroom.

Contemplating taking her first step forward, and sincerely worried about falling flat on her face, Tiffany suddenly felt a strong, muscular arm go around her waist, keeping her upright.

She caught just the slightest whiff of familiar cologne.

Eddie.

"I'm fine," she protested halfheartedly, attempting to shrug him off—or at least thinking that she was shrugging him off.

"No argument about that," he agreed jovially. "But you're also wobbly at the moment, and a face-plant on the asphalt might be rather painful, not to mention it might really scare some of the younger kids.

Don't fight this," he told her, when she tried to glare at him. "Just let me help you to your classroom. I promise you'll get the feeling back in your legs in a few minutes."

"So now you're a doctor?" she asked, trying to sound sarcastic, but in fact barely managing to eek out the question.

"No, but what I am is an amateur runner," Eddie answered.

Tiffany sighed, surrendering. She would have loved to just pull away from him, but knew she was a lot better off accepting his help for now.

After a moment, as they made their way to the school building, she asked, "Is there anything that you're not good at?"

"Yeah," he told her without any hesitation as he spared her a meaningful glance. "Apparently making friends with you." Keeping his arm tightly around her waist, he followed the others into the building.

Tiffany tried to square her shoulders, as if bracing herself against him, but she failed.

"We don't need to be friends," she informed Eddie. She was doing her best not to be aware of the way his arm felt around her waist, or the fact that he was holding her close to keep her from falling.

At least that was the excuse he was using to have his arm around her, she grudgingly thought.

"Right," Eddie responded cryptically. "Why be friends when we've got our rivalry to keep us warm? Or at least that's what you think." He stopped in front of her classroom door. "Looks like we're home, Toto." He thought of escorting her all the way into the room and helping her to her chair, but had a feeling she would balk at that, so he stopped where he was. "See you when the next twister passes through." With a grin, he slipped his arm from around her waist.

Tiffany frowned. "Half the time I don't know what you're talking about," she accused.

He didn't rise to the bait or grow defensive the way she expected him to. Instead, he grinned that bone-melting grin of his that was *really* getting to her, and cheerfully said, "Always leave them guessing, that's what someone once told me."

"That refers to Saturday morning cliffhangers and quiz shows," she retorted. And then, because he *had* gone out of his way and he clearly didn't have to, she mumbled "Thanks" before she made her way inside her classroom, careful to hold on to the wall as she went.

Reaching her desk, she eased herself into her chair and exhaled a huge sigh of relief. Only then did she realize that her students, all sitting in their seats, were almost as quiet as the occupants of a cemetery. They were looking right at her.

She knew what they were thinking. "I'm not used to running," Tiffany told them honestly.

It was rather obvious, but kids liked having the obvious spelled out for them. They also appreciated having adults regard them as equals, and in sharing her "secret" with them the way she just did, that put them on a different footing than just teacher-and-students.

"You ran pretty good for someone who doesn't," Jorge Ramos told her with glowing approval.

Where did she begin to untangle that sentence? While she appreciated the sentiment behind the awkward comment, it was her job as his teacher to try to get Jorge to use better English.

"I ran *well*," she corrected.

"You think so, too, huh?" Danny asked, adding his voice to the discussion.

It took everything Tiffany had not to roll her eyes at the boy's response. But he meant well. All the kids she'd encountered in her teaching career so far meant well. That was why she kept coming back, year after year, to do this, to touch young minds and try to help them develop. There was something almost magical about it. It certainly felt mystical at times.

"You've got great form, Jorge, but we have *got* to work on improving your English," she told him with a kindly laugh.

Jorge was about to protest that he already knew English when he was interrupted by the sound of chimes coming over the PA system.

Everyone's attention instantly shifted to the announcement they were all waiting for. The announcement telling them which class had won the race and how much money the school had managed to raise for the local shelter.

That number came first, and when Mrs. Walters told them the amount, a cheer went up in Tiffany's classroom that was heartily echoed throughout the rest of the school.

After a couple minutes, the classes settled down to await what they considered to be the "big" news. It wasn't long in coming.

"After carefully going over the number of laps that were tallied by each student in his or her class, I am happy to announce the outcome of Bedford Elementary's very first annual Race for the Shelter."

The principal paused at that point and Tiffany knew it was for effect, but she really wished that Mrs. Walters would get this over with.

"Boys and girls, I'm happy to say that it looks like there were will be *two* classes going on a picnic to William Mason Park next Friday, because we have a tie," she declared with no small measure of enthusiasm. "Mr. Montoya's class and Ms. Lee's class both did an outstanding job today. Each class ran a record-breaking total of 750 laps. I hope you all join me in giving each class—and yourselves—a great big round of applause. You're all awesome, each and every one of you, and I am proud to be your principal. Now go home, all of you, and hit the showers," she instructed with an amused laugh. "School's dismissed!"

The words barely had time to sink in. The second that they did, Tiffany's students jumped to their feet. They grabbed their backpacks and, holding on to them tightly, made a beeline for the classroom door in what amounted to record-breaking time.

Still not trusting her legs, Tiffany remained in her chair. "Great job, everybody," she called out to her students as they hurried out the door. "I'm proud of each and every one of you!"

"You did good, too, Ms. Lee," Danny told her, just before he ran out of the classroom.

"*Well*, Danny," she repeated, in a voice she knew he wouldn't hear. "I did *well*."

Tiffany sighed and shook her head. Obviously she was going to have to tutor that boy, too. Better yet, maybe she needed to double up on the class's English lessons.

She continued to sit there for a few minutes longer, trying to gather her strength. She was consciously searching for enough energy to make it to her car on her own, without weaving.

Thinking back, she couldn't remember the last time she had felt this drained. Not even when she and Eddie had gotten that tub up to the second floor.

And then she quietly laughed to herself as she shook her head incredulously. Why was it that all her moments of being completely exhausted seemed to somehow be tied to Montoya?

The next second she realized that she should have gotten herself together sooner—and faster—because Eddie was there, standing in the doorway of her classroom.

A nightmare come to life.

"I wasn't sure if I'd still find you here," he said as he walked in.

"Why would you be looking for me?" she asked. "It's a tie, so our bet is null and void."

He laughed off her statement. "I wouldn't be looking to collect any money from you even if it hadn't been a tie."

Tiffany frowned. The way he put it, it sounded as if Montoya believed that if they hadn't tied, he would have been the one to win the bet. It figured. The man's ego was apparently as large as he was.

She felt her back going up. "So why are you here?"

His face was the very picture of innocence as he answered, "I wanted to congratulate you."

She pressed her lips together and sighed. Damn it,

was he really a better person than she was? "I suppose I should be congratulating you, too."

Eddie shrugged casually. "Only if you want to."

More goodness, she thought, trying to hold on to her fraying temper. "Don't make this difficult," she told him.

"I wouldn't dream of it," he responded. And then he smiled, lowering his head so that his lips were close to her ear as he whispered, "You do know we're on the same side, don't you?"

Tiffany thought of all the times they had been pitted against one another throughout college. She felt as if they had always been at odds and butting heads during those years. There was no doubt in her mind that if they had known one another longer, they would have been competitive that much longer, as well.

"And just how do you figure that?" she demanded.

"Well, we both want to give these kids the best education we possibly can. Give them the best experience at school so that they're as well equipped to face the future as we can possibly make them." Eddie saw the expression on her face. How could someone so beautiful look so far from happy? he wondered. "Did I say something wrong?"

She hated to admit this, but in all honesty, she knew she had to. "No, you didn't. You're right," she told him, trying not to grit her teeth. "You're absolutely right."

Eddie grinned. "And you want to pound on me for that," he guessed.

Tiffany thought of denying what he'd just said, but that would be lying. Besides, he somehow seemed to know when she lied. So she answered truthfully, "With all my heart and soul."

She thought that would take Eddie aback. She certainly didn't expect him to laugh, but he did. He laughed a great deal and with gusto.

"I didn't say anything funny," she said almost defensively.

He could barely get the words out in between the laughter. "I'm just envisioning you trying to beat me to a pulp."

She stared at him. "And that's funny?" she questioned.

"Yeah," he told her, finally getting himself under control. "It kind of is."

And then Eddie really surprised her with what he said next. "Have dinner with me, Tiffany."

Chapter Fourteen

Totally stunned, Tiffany could only stare at the man in her classroom. She was unable to summon any words from her mouth.

After a moment, Eddie laughed again, totally amused. "Wow, I had no idea it was so easy to render you speechless. I should have asked you out to dinner years ago."

Drawing a breath, Tiffany was finally able to find her tongue. "I wouldn't have gone," she informed him flatly. "I was too poor back then to afford a food taster."

Eddie's generous mouth only curved further. "What would have made you think you needed one?"

She couldn't help wondering if he had a totally different memory of those four years when they had been in the same classes together.

"The fact that we were always at odds, always competing, always—" She stopped abruptly. "Want me to go on?"

He appeared completely unaffected by what she was saying. "For as long as you like, as long as you say yes to dinner."

Wasn't anything getting through to that thick head of his? "Then I'd better stop talking."

"Oh, c'mon, Tiffany." Instead of leaving, he came closer and perched on the edge of her desk. "What's wrong with a little celebratory meal between two educators who not only successfully urged on their classes to do their very best, but managed to get those two classes to raise a very nice sum of money that will go a long way toward helping a lot of deserving single parents and their children?"

"That was a hell of a long sentence," she observed with a touch of sarcasm. When he didn't seem to rise to the bait, she wavered a little. "Well, I guess if you put it that way…"

Maybe she was being a bit too standoffish. After all, Montoya was only suggesting sharing a meal in a public place. Technically, they *did* have something to celebrate. And anyway, how long could grabbing a quick meal take?

Eddie didn't need to hear any more. "Great. I'll pick you up at six tonight."

"Tonight?" she repeated. She hadn't expected him to act on his invitation so quickly. "No, make it tomorrow night," she said, backing off a little. "I'm too exhausted to go out tonight."

He didn't want to push her. Frankly, he was rather stunned that she'd actually agreed.

"Tomorrow," he echoed, then regarded her a little more thoughtfully. "That'll give you an extra twenty-four hours to come up with an excuse why you're not going."

"Think optimistically," Tiffany suggested, although he did have a very valid point. "That gives me an extra twenty-four hours to talk myself *into* going out with you."

Eddie laughed drily. "I'm an optimist, not a simpleton," he told her. "But since I can't exactly tie you up and strap you to the roof of my car, tomorrow it is."

And with that, he walked out of her classroom, leaving her to contemplate her temporary descent into insanity.

Why had she agreed?

"What are you *doing*?" Tiffany asked the young woman who was staring back at her in the mirror the next afternoon. "Have you completely lost your mind? Why are you going out with this guy?"

Disgusted, she tossed aside the dress she had pulled out of her closet and held up to herself. A dusty shade of emerald green, it was one of her favorites and she'd actually thought about wearing it tonight. It landed haphazardly on the bed.

"Yes, when it comes to good-looking, on a scale of one to ten the guy's a twelve, but so what? Neil was good-looking, remember?" she asked her reflection. "So good-looking that there were always flocks of girls fluttering around him. Girls he didn't bother shooing away," she stressed. "Remember that?"

Neil Cavell had made it past all her natural defenses in astonishing time. A newly minted lawyer high on his own abilities, Neil had pursued her until she'd finally gone out with him. And then he'd pulled out all the stops. Before she knew it, she was falling in love with him. And when he proposed a few short months later, Tiffany was certain that she had beaten the odds and found someone to spend the rest of her life with.

What she hadn't realized was that along with his good looks, superior intelligence and magnetic personality, her Prince Charming also had the morals of an alley cat on shore leave.

The first time she caught Neil cheating on her, he called it a one-time thing and swore to her that it would never happen again. He did the same thing the second time she caught him cheating. By the third time, she knew that he was incapable of telling the truth or remaining faithful for the length of time it took to spell the word *fidelity*.

Right then and there, as she threw his engagement ring at him and ordered him to get out of her life, Tiffany had sworn she would never allow herself to be in that position again, never surrender her heart so that it could be shattered.

Excising all reminders of Neil out of her life had been painful as well as hard. Telling her mother that there wouldn't be a wedding and that Neil was now history had been downright excruciating.

"And the way to keep that from ever happening again is to never take that first step toward letting someone get his foot in the door," she told her reflection. "Never let him in at all. Agreed?"

She could have sworn that her reflection appeared to look just the slightest bit sad at the prospect of closing this partially cracked open door. But it would be best if she told Eddie that she had changed her mind and decided not to go out with him. Even if it was just for an innocent dinner.

Heaven knew, she had enough in her life as it was. She had her students and she had her family. If she got lonely, there were sisters she could call, nieces and nephews she could play with. If she needed a man to help her out—and those occasions were really few and far between—she had four brothers-in-law to turn to.

She had made peace with the fact that despite the crush she had so long ago, there was no happily ever after, no Prince Charming.

She was just fine the way she was, Tiffany told herself. Perfectly—

She froze.

That was the doorbell.

Eddie.

Tiffany braced herself. She hadn't called him to cancel dinner because she knew she'd get caught up in an extra-long back and forth "discussion" that would undoubtedly lead nowhere. The man could argue a statue to death. Turning him away at her front door had the kind of finality to it that she found both appealing and satisfying.

Her refusal prepared and ready to go, Tiffany marched to the front door and threw it open.

She started talking the second she saw him. "I'm sorry, Eddie, but as it turns out I really don't feel up to going out for dinner."

She expected him to take her refusal in stride, possibly even say something cryptic, and then just leave. She did *not* expect him to grin.

"I had a feeling you'd say that," Eddie told her. Then, instead of turning away and leaving, he walked right into her house.

Hadn't he heard her? Turning around and following him inside, she raised her voice and told him, "I said I didn't feel up to going out."

"I know," he replied. "Like I said, I had a feeling you'd say that—which is why I brought a home-cooked meal with me." He indicated the two shopping bags he was holding. "We," he informed her, "are dining in."

"A home-cooked meal," she echoed incredulously, staring at him as if he had just said they were going to build a submarine together in her living room.

"Yes. I'll just get everything set up in your kitchen," he told her. And with that, he made his way there.

Flabbergasted, Tiffany had no choice but to follow him again. "You had your mother cook us a meal?" she asked in disbelief. Just how much did the woman want to get rid of her son?

Setting both shopping bags on the counter, Eddie turned to face her. "My mother?" he echoed incredulously. "Why would you think my mother cooked this?"

"Because that looks like a lot of food," Tiffany said, nodding at the two bags. "And you said it was home cooked. For most men a home-cooked meal means boiling a couple of hot dogs and sticking them into buns."

"I guess I'm not like most men then," Eddie responded.

She was *not* about to get caught in that little trap, wasn't about to comment one way or another on his supposed "uniqueness."

Instead, she challenged his honesty. "You're saying you cooked an actual dinner."

"That's what I'm saying," he answered. And then, because she still looked so skeptical, he backed up his statement. "I grew up in a houseful of women. I couldn't help but learn how to cook practically by osmosis," he told her. "Especially when my mother taught Elena, the sister who couldn't boil water.

"I'm not saying that I prepared a feast, but it's definitely a cut above boiled hot dogs and buns," he promised. "Now sit down—" he nodded toward the table "—and prepare to be fed."

Instead of doing what he told her to do, Tiffany began to cross to the cabinets. "We need dishes."

"Actually," he said, catching hold of her wrist and stopping her, "we don't. All we need are two forks."

She looked at him, puzzled. A less than flattering image ran through her mind. "We're going to feed out of a trough?"

Instead of getting insulted, Eddie merely laughed. "No wonder you're such a good teacher. You have a very colorful imagination. But to answer your question, no, we're not feeding out of a trough. I prepared individual servings of quiche. The whole meal is contained in a pie tin. When you finish, there'll be nothing to wash except the fork."

She had to admit that sounded rather appealing. "You seem to have thought of everything."

He grinned as he placed the two servings of quiche

Lorraine on the table and then retrieved two forks out of the silverware drawer.

"Another dividend of growing up in a houseful of women," he told her. After sitting down opposite Tiffany, he picked up his fork and said, "Dig in!"

She didn't want to like it. More than anything, she wanted to find fault with the meal Montoya had prepared.

But she couldn't.

Accustomed to good food, she still had to admit that the quiche Lorraine Eddie had made was in a class of its own.

Although he made no reference to it, she knew that Eddie was waiting for her to say something about the meal he had prepared for them. She resisted for as long as she could. Finally, she placed the fork beside the now empty individual pie tin and, after sighing, surrendered and told him, almost against her will, "It was very good."

"You don't sound very happy about that," Eddie observed, amused.

"I'm not," she told him honestly. "I'm waiting for you to be bad at something. Why aren't you bad at something?" she asked accusingly.

To his credit, Eddie didn't laugh. "Just lucky I guess," he responded carelessly. "Maybe you won't like the apple pie I made."

Tiffany rolled her eyes as she sighed again. This was just too much. "You made pie." The next moment she took heart in the thought that maybe he was actually kidding. Cooking was one thing, being accomplished at baking as well was quite another.

Eddie shrugged in response, as if it was no big

deal. "Well, I thought that since the oven was already on, why not?"

He *wasn't* kidding, she realized, mentally throwing up her hands. "Sure, why not?"

About to get up, Eddie stopped and regarded her for a long moment. "Why is it so important to you that I fail at something?"

"Maybe because when something is too good to be true, it isn't." She didn't know how to explain it any better than that.

"I'm not too good to be true, Tiffany," Eddie pointed out. "I just try really hard, that's all."

He finally rose from the table and cleared away the empty tins. Then he took the apple pie out of the second shopping bag. After placing it temporarily on the counter, he took two small plates from the cabinet and brought them, along with the pie, to the table.

"I could say the same about you, you know," he told her as he cut two slices, placing them on plates and then putting one in front of her and the other in front of him. He made himself comfortable and sat back down opposite her.

"Say what about me?" she asked, after waiting in vain for him to conclude his statement.

She wanted to resist sampling the pie he'd set in front of her, but it was still warm enough to waft its aroma toward her, all but making her mouth water. He had to have taken the pie out of the oven just before he came here.

There was no getting away from it. The man was incredible.

"That you're too good to be true," he told her casually.

"Yeah, right," Tiffany all but jeered.

He put down his fork for a moment and made his case. "When your students asked you to run with them," he pointed out, "you didn't turn them down and you didn't just run a lap or two to placate them. You ran as long as there was even *one* of your students still in the race. Not because you're a natural runner—" he grinned as if he was sharing a private joke "—because I watched you and your form says you're definitely *not* a natural runner. But because they asked and you wanted to encourage them. So you went outside of your comfort zone and you ran. That's pretty perfect in my book."

She laughed rather skeptically. "That must be a very small book."

Eddie surprised her by saying, "It is." And then, his eyes on hers, he went on to say, "Because perfection isn't that easy to find."

Why did it feel like everything had just stopped at that moment? Even her refrigerator, which was given to humming a good part of the time, had suddenly ceased making a sound.

It was as if some giant, unseen hand had just pressed a pause button and everything had.

Everything but her heart, which seemed to have launched into double time.

"This is very good pie," Tiffany heard herself telling him, because she was suddenly desperate to say *something*.

"Thanks. Apple pie is pretty easy, actually," Eddie replied modestly. "I was thinking of making tiramisu, but ran out of time," he confided. "Next time," he promised.

That caught her completely off guard.

"Next time?" she repeated, feeling as if the words were suddenly falling from her lips in cartoon-like slow motion.

"Yes. Unless you want to be the one to make the dessert," he told her.

Except for scrambled eggs and toast, she was a total disaster in the kitchen when it came to doing anything but cleaning it.

"I'd rather not have to call the paramedics," she murmured.

His smile was nothing if not encouraging. "It can't be that bad."

"It's not that good, either," she admitted.

It was supposed to be a flat, flippant denial, but she just couldn't seem to get her head in gear because her mind was currently focused elsewhere.

It was focused on the way Eddie's lips moved when he spoke.

Tiffany rose to her feet, thinking that she would make a getaway, or at least offer some sort of an excuse and slip into the bathroom, away from him. But he rose with her, and suddenly, she wasn't going anywhere.

At least not without her lips, and they were currently occupied. More specifically, they were pressing against his.

Chapter Fifteen

She wanted to say that Eddie had made the first move, but the truth was she really didn't know if he had, or if *she* had been the one to set the wheels in motion.

Tiffany didn't know if she had, without warning, just given in to the intense curiosity of finding out what his lips tasted like, pressed up against hers.

But there she was, in the middle of an apple-pie-flavored kiss, her head spinning the way it would have had she just consumed more than her share of a very potent, intoxicating wine.

The kiss took her prisoner.

Tiffany was only vaguely aware of lacing her arms around his neck, of standing up on her very tiptoes to further deepen a kiss that was already so deep she couldn't begin to touch bottom.

Eddie's arms slipped about her waist and she felt her body being pressed against his, along with flashes of electricity dancing through her.

After what seemed like a breathtaking, delicious eternity, she felt his mouth leaving hers, felt him draw back just enough to allow a sliver of space to be created between them.

The smile on his lips filtered through her like sunshine and his eyes met hers.

"That is a hell of a better dessert than any pie I could have baked," he told her.

She was swiftly losing ground. Tiffany was weakening as her heart pounded like a drum solo. Any second now, she would wind up throwing herself at him, and no good could come of that.

"Maybe you'd better leave," she told him in a voice barely above a whisper.

She didn't want him to, but was afraid she would wind up capitulating to her own desires in record time if he remained.

Eddie nodded, knowing that if he stayed any longer, things might just start progressing too fast, and he did *not* want to scare Tiffany away. It had taken him a while to come this far and he was not about to risk losing ground.

"Maybe I'd better," he agreed, albeit reluctantly. He paused only long enough to softly press his lips to her forehead. "Thanks for the pleasure of your company."

Oh damn, Tiffany thought. *Why did he have to act so nice?* She could handle a competitive Eddie, *welcomed* a competitive Eddie. But a "nice" Eddie had her sinking into quicksand.

"I'll see you Monday," he told her as he began to leave the kitchen.

"You're forgetting the pie," she prompted, noticing that Eddie had left the tin of homemade dessert on the table.

Tiffany quickly moved toward it. Taking one of the shopping bags, she began to pack up the pie.

Eddie turned to look at her over his shoulder. "No, I'm not. Keep it. I made it for you," he reminded her.

Her hands dropped to her sides.

Tiffany watched him turn away again, watched him walk into the living room and then toward the front door.

He was really leaving.

That was when her resolve finally broke apart like a tree house in a hurricane.

Tiffany heard herself calling after him, hardly believing what she was doing. What she was *about* to do. But she just couldn't stop herself.

"Eddie."

He paused and once again turned to look at her. "Yes?"

"Don't go." The next moment, Tiffany flew from the kitchen to the front door. In case he hadn't heard her, she repeated, "Don't go."

He needed nothing more than that.

Catching her up in his arms, Eddie kissed her again. And again. Kissed her long and hard until there was no doubt left for either of them.

He wasn't going anywhere, except on an emotional journey that in his opinion had been a very long time in coming.

As Eddie held her in his arms, one kiss flowered

into another, each one longer than the last. Each one deeper than the last, until all they knew was the heat of their desire for one another and the unexplored world that was waiting for them to enter.

Tiffany's pulse was racing.

This all felt new and wondrous to her, and yet at the same time it was somehow beautifully familiar. Something in her soul had been waiting her whole life for this, knowing it would come, impatient for it to finally make its appearance.

She couldn't quite explain it.

Tiffany's head continued to spin as an eagerness seized her, held her fast and urged her on to every new step she took. Made her crave crossing each new threshold.

Although he desperately wanted to satiate this untamed desire he was experiencing, Eddie deliberately held himself in check so that he would take this slow. He didn't want to frighten her, didn't want to scare Tiffany away, and he felt if he pressed too hard, if he went too fast, that would be the end result: she'd be frightened off and then he would never know what it really meant to be with her the way he had thought about for so very long.

So he feasted on her lips before slowly moving on to her throat and then to each of her shoulders, gently tugging away clothing that got in his way.

And then, finally, there was nothing left in his way. Nothing but the exhilarating feel of her warm, pliant skin beneath his reverent, caressing hands, beneath his eager lips.

Tiffany had urgently pulled away his clothing as

he stripped away hers, freeing him to feel the heat of her body as she twisted and turned against him. She surrendered herself to him, to the demands that this passion-laced moment had placed on both of them.

Somewhere along the line Eddie simply ceased strategizing and just gave himself up to the moment and to the woman who had somehow managed to snare him securely in her grasp while he had been busy planning to win her over.

Complicated plans fell by the wayside as Eddie gave himself up to the feel of her, to the passion that was beating wildly within him like the wings of a frantic hummingbird trying to gain the sky.

She couldn't seem to get enough of him.

Every touch, every kiss made her want Eddie that much more. Made her want this to continue that much more, whatever "this" actually was—other than just a total and complete madness of the blood.

The more he kissed and touched her, the more she wanted him to.

She didn't want this to ever stop.

Tiffany felt utterly insatiable and so not like herself, but this was no time to puzzle things out, to attempt to be logical about something that was, at bottom, so very *il*logical.

So she allowed herself to just enjoy it, to tell herself that whatever happened tomorrow would happen tomorrow.

But *now* was for loving and for experiencing all that there was to experience from this lovemaking that was sweeping her off her feet.

Eddie had begun this heady trip into desire's playground holding back in order not to frighten her, but now her sweeping displays of passion were all but leaving him behind in the dust.

It was all he could do to keep up with her.

And then, when she reciprocated and branded his body with soft, openmouthed kisses the way he had branded hers, Eddie knew he could no longer hold himself in check. He wanted her *now. Needed* her now with a overwhelming craving the likes of which he had never felt before.

Shifting Tiffany so that she was suddenly beneath him on the thick throw rug on the floor, Eddie slid his body up along hers until he was looming directly over her, his eyes on hers.

He wasn't sure if he could read what was there, only that he loved looking into her eyes. Loved feeling himself getting lost in them.

His heart swelled as he slowly parted her legs and then entered her. He almost lost his concentration when she raised her hips up to his, but at the last moment, he regained his tight control over himself. With slow precision he began to move, causing her to echo the rhythm until they moved together as one to the increasingly more frantic beat that only they were able to hear.

They urged one another on, faster and faster, until they were suddenly skydiving off the top of the summit they had just conquered.

Together, their bodies hot and sealed to one another, they experienced the ultimate moment.

The anticipated fireworks came, bathing them both in the outburst.

Eddie held her tightly against him as the cavalcade

of lights exploded, then little by little, receded into the shadows before vanishing altogether.

And still he held her against him. Held her as Tiffany felt the wild beating of his heart against hers, held her as the madness receded and sanity slowly tiptoed back.

He could feel her breathing returning to normal as the warmth of each breath seeped into his chest. He waited for what he thought was the inevitable. Any second now, he expected her to pull away, maybe even murmur that she had temporarily gone insane and that if he breathed a word of what had happened here to anyone, she would have no choice but to cut his heart out.

He waited, but the inevitable was taking its time in making its appearance.

She didn't say a word.

Finally, concerned, he softly said her name. "Tiffany?"

"Hmmm?"

Her breath was still tickling his chest. He felt a renewed surge of desire, but did his best to block it out. "Is everything all right?"

She sighed softly before answering him.

"Well, other than the fact that black is white and up is down, yes, everything's all right." Tiffany raised her head then, the ends of her silky hair lightly gliding along his chest, tantalizing him all over again. His stomach tightened. Her eyes met his. "Why?" she asked.

He kept his arm around her, although not nearly as tightly as before. He didn't want her feeling trapped. "I just thought that, well, you know…"

His voice trailed off because he just didn't know what to say, or how to even finish his thought in a satisfactory manner. The last thing he wanted to do was affront her. He didn't want her to think this was just a casual coupling, but at the same time, he didn't want to put any pressure on her if she chose to attach no significance to what had just happened between them.

The fact that he did couldn't be allowed to figure into this right now. Because "right now" was all about her and not about him.

Her happiness meant that much to him.

He heard Tiffany laugh softly. "You know, for an accomplished, articulate man, you seem oddly at a loss for words," she observed.

"That's because you've managed to reduce my mind to a smoldering pile of rubble," he told her. "I can't even form a coherent sentence."

"Is that so?" she pretended to ask innocently.

Eddie took his cue from her, relaxing a little as he did so. "I'm afraid that's so."

A hint of mischief entered her eyes. "Well, then maybe the universe is trying to tell you something."

"And exactly what is it that the universe is trying to tell me?" he asked, doing his best to keep a straight face.

She moved her body a tad closer to his, eliminating any and all space as another fire began to ignite between them. "That maybe this isn't the time for sentences, coherent or otherwise."

His breath caught in his throat. This was better than he could have ever possibly imagined. "And just what is it the time for?"

"This," she answered, slipping her hand seductively along his chest as she brought her mouth down on his again, recreating that first spark and immediately allowing it to ignite into something hot and intensely fierce.

Except that this time it went a lot faster. The path was quickly engulfed in flames that were a direct result of the desire that took root between them as well as *in* them.

Deep down, Tiffany sensed that she would regret this. That she would relive it and upbraid herself for giving in to her desire.

Not once, but twice.

But all that was to be faced and dealt with later. For now, all she wanted to do was enjoy it. To pretend that she still believed in "happily ever after" the way she once had when she'd first fallen in love and fell victim to making plans that included the words *marriage* and *forever*. More than anything, she wanted to pretend that she didn't know what she *did* know now.

And to believe, with all her heart, that what she was experiencing could be as real and as pure as she wished with all her heart.

They made love throughout the evening and into the night. And when they were too exhausted to do anything more than just breathe, they did that while holding on to one another and holding on to the fragments of the dreams they were both still capable of having.

The little voice in Tiffany's head did its best to make her come to her senses. It admonished her, because she had done everything that she had promised herself never to do again.

The problem was she had enjoyed it far more than she had ever thought she could.

Certainly more than she had when she'd been with Neil.

It was as if she had taken a quantum leap into a world she hadn't believed existed.

With all her heart, she wished she could make it last. That she could make this feeling and the reasons behind it continue. But fairy tales belonged in books, not in everyday life, and she was oh-so-painfully aware of that.

Still, she was reluctant to release her hold on the shreds of her dreams that she still held so firmly in her hands.

Desperate to put off the inevitable, Tiffany did the only thing she could think of to preserve the illusion just a little bit longer.

She pretended to be asleep.

And after a while, the need to pretend ceased to exist because the pretense became reality.

Chapter Sixteen

Tiffany stretched as sleep receded. Her arm came in contact with nothing.

Her eyes flew open.

She was alone.

The place beside her in bed was empty. She felt a tiny sliver of relief, but at the same time, a deep bereavement washed over her, all but drowning her.

She was relieved because this meant she didn't have to come up with any awkward, morning-after small talk, and bereft because there was no one to talk to. Only an emptiness echoed back at her.

"Okay," she told herself sternly, "no feeling sorry for yourself. As far as evenings went, it was a surprisingly good one. And now it's a new day, time to put one foot in front of the other and move on with your life. This *is* life," she insisted. "Not a fairy tale. You know that."

"Who are you talking to?"

Tiffany screamed. Screamed because she'd been certain she was alone and Eddie had just stuck his head into her bedroom and asked her a question. He'd nearly caused her to jump out of her skin.

Pressing her hand against her chest to keep her heart in place, Tiffany cried, "What are you doing here?"

"You ever notice that you keep asking me that question?" Eddie pointed out, amused. "By now you should really have a bead on the answer."

She blew out a breath as her heart began to settle down. "I thought you'd left."

The look on his face said that her assumption was way off base.

"I wouldn't have left without saying goodbye. I was downstairs, making you breakfast," he explained, then added, "I know that scrambled eggs and toast are your area of expertise, but I thought I'd surprise you by giving you a break and serving you breakfast in bed." He waved his hands. "Except now you've spoiled the surprise, so you might as well come on downstairs and have breakfast in the kitchen—after you put on something, of course." His smile widened. "Unless you'd rather come down just the way you are."

That was when Tiffany saw that she wasn't wearing anything. A night of lovemaking had rendered clothing utterly unnecessary, and when he'd walked in and made her almost fall out of bed, she'd completely forgotten that she was still nude.

Painfully aware of her lack of clothing now, she

turned a bright shade of pink and made a grab for the bed sheet, pulling it against her.

"I'll get dressed," she said, each word sticking to the inside of her suddenly very dry mouth.

"Spoilsport," Eddie teased, laughter entering his eyes. "I'll just go downstairs and wait for you."

The moment he left the room, Tiffany quickly got dressed, doing her best not to dwell on the fact that she'd been naked in front of him—and that he hadn't given her any indication of her oversight until the very end. Yes, they had made love last night, but somehow having him see her like this in the light of day felt totally different.

She just wasn't going to think about it. Otherwise, she wouldn't get through breakfast. Worse than that, she wouldn't be able to look Eddie in the eye ever again or even be around him at work.

Damn, how had this happened? she silently demanded, before pushing her bare feet into a pair of sandals and heading downstairs. She was supposed to be more aware of her surroundings than this. And definitely more in control of herself.

Even before she reached the bottom of the stairs, Tiffany could smell it. Smell the very tempting aroma of breakfast seductively rising up to meet her. Reminding her that she was hungry. She was one of those people who woke up immediately ready to eat first thing in the morning, no period of adjustment necessary.

And this did smell *very* good.

"Morning," Eddie said, smiling brightly at her as if he hadn't just been upstairs and seen her five minutes ago in all her nude glory. "You're just in time for breakfast," he told her cheerfully.

"Yes, I know. You mentioned making breakfast when you came into my bedroom," Tiffany murmured, avoiding his eyes as she sat down in front of the plate of sunny-side-up eggs and toast.

"Bedroom?" Eddie repeated innocently. He placed a hot cup of coffee next to her plate. "I don't remember coming into your bedroom."

She started to tell him to drop the act when she realized that it *was* an act and that he was doing it for her. Whether it was to spare her embarrassment or to just place less emphasis on that uncomfortable moment when she'd realized that she was nude, she didn't know. But she appreciated the thoughtfulness that had prompted this little charade on his part.

Was he really as nice as he seemed, or was she in for a very rude awakening?

Once burned, twice leery, and Neil had made her very, very leery.

"Why don't you start eating before it gets cold?" Eddie suggested as he took his seat opposite her, setting down his own plate and cup of coffee. He began to dig in himself.

She watched him for a moment. He ate with almost boyish enthusiasm. Maybe she'd been wrong about Eddie. Maybe he actually *was* a good guy, she thought.

And maybe you're just jumping to conclusions, that little logical voice in her head hissed. *Remember Neil? He seemed like a good guy and you recall how that turned out.*

Tiffany pressed her lips together, torn between wanting to think the best of the man sitting across from her—the man who had managed to rock the foundations of her very world last night—and remaining on her guard because she remembered just how painful it was trying to regroup after having her heart almost literally ripped out of her chest.

"Something wrong with the eggs?" Eddie asked. "You're not really eating," he observed.

Someday, she was going to have to develop a poker face. But obviously not today.

"No, I'm just thinking about the picnic," Tiffany answered, grasping at the first thing that came to her mind.

"Well, since both our classes are going, it'll be a join effort," Eddie reminded her, finishing off his toast. "Don't worry, everything'll be okay," he assured her.

Don't worry, everything'll be okay...

His words echoed in her head, but she remained unconvinced. The joint picnic might turn out all right, but would she? Tiffany couldn't help wondering.

Because she knew Eddie was looking at her, she forced a smile to her face. But that did nothing to loosen the knot in her stomach.

Everything was not *going to be okay,* Tiffany thought uneasily.

The much anticipated picnic for the two winning classes took place the following Wednesday.

All the students involved arrived early and the very air seemed charged with their exuberance. An enthusiasm that was challenged almost right from the very beginning.

The forecast was for another sunny, picture-perfect California day. Tiffany had checked two different weather sources before coming to school, just to be sure.

Getting out of her car, she crossed over to Eddie, who was already there and talking to the two mothers who had volunteered to come along on the trip. She glanced up at the sky as she approached the adults. Far from being sunny, the sky was overcast and some of the clouds looked as if they were darkening.

Tiffany frowned. It just couldn't rain today.

"Looks like the weather bureau failed to tell someone that it's supposed to be bright and sunny today," she commented as she walked up to them.

"It'll clear up," Eddie told her. "It hardly ever rains this time of year in Southern California."

Tiffany glanced up doubtfully one last time. "I'll hold you to that."

"Do we get to pick our bus?" one of Eddie's students asked eagerly.

"No, but Ms. Lee and I do." He looked at all the upturned, eager faces of his third graders. "And I picked that one," he announced, pointing to the first bus that had pulled up.

Because there were a total of fifty-eight students, two school buses had been requested to transport them to the park. Eddie had been on the school grounds since before the buses arrived and had already talked to both drivers, reviewing the intended destination and what was on the day's agenda.

"We're getting on in an orderly fashion, aren't we, class?" he asked, raising his voice above the high-pitched bits and pieces of conversation flying through the air.

"Yes, Mr. Montoya," his class responded, lowering their voices just a little.

Eddie stood next to the bus's open doors, directing them onto the bus in single file. Once the last of the students got on—as well as one volunteer mother— he got on himself.

Tiffany had done the same with her class, taking a head count of her students as they climbed on the bus. By the time she got on, she noticed that her fifth graders had immediately made themselves comfortable. Their eagerness was palatable. Her volunteer parent was sitting in the middle. Surprisingly, there were still a few empty seats to be had.

"All right, everyone, listen up. I want you all to be on your very best behavior. Once we get to the picnic area, no wandering off by yourselves—or even in pairs," she added quickly, when she saw one of the boys raise his hand. "We want you all to have fun on this trip—but not so much fun that this winds up being the last field trip Bedford Elementary ever has, understood?" she asked, her eyes sweeping over her class.

"Understood," her students responded, their voices out of sync.

"Okay." Satisfied that they were all seated, she turned to the driver. "Let's close the doors and get going!"

The doors closed just as she requested. It was the second part of her order that was giving the driver trouble. Each attempt to start the engine ended with it emitting a grinding noise that sounded very much as if the bus's gears were giving up the ghost.

After a fourth attempt to start it failed, the bus

driver turned to look at Tiffany, a befuddled expression on his gaunt face.

"I'm not sure what's wrong," he told her, sounding highly irritated. "I'm going to call in and see if I can get them to send out another bus to replace this one."

Tiffany was by nature an optimist, but this situation didn't look very promising. She'd heard something about there being cutbacks in all sorts of school-related departments.

That meant buses, as well.

"Do you think you can actually get one at this late hour?" she asked, because as far as securing transportation went, the hour was definitely late.

The driver ran his hand over his bald head and looked at her sheepishly. "Frankly, no."

That news was met with a loud chorus of groans. The students had been hanging on every word exchanged between her and the bus driver. Tiffany knew that they were counting on this outing and she hated disappointing them, but there was no way she could pull a bus out of a hat.

As she attempted to settle her class down, she heard knocking on the bus's closed doors. Turning, she saw that Eddie was standing just outside.

"Open your doors," she immediately instructed the driver.

Eddie made no attempt to step inside once the doors swung wide. Instead, he asked the driver, "What's wrong? We saw that you weren't following us when we started to drive away from the school."

Meaning *he* saw, Tiffany thought. Eddie had to have been the one to stop the other driver and have the driver return. She was reluctantly beginning to appreciate this man more and more.

"Something's wrong with the bus," one of her students called out.

"We're not going to get to go to the picnic," another lamented.

Several others were quick to join in expressing their disappointment.

Eddie held his hands up for silence, and to Tiffany's amazement, that was exactly what he got. Immediately. "Sure, you're going on the picnic," he told them.

The bus driver interrupted, lowering his voice. "I already told this teacher—" he nodded toward Tiffany "—that we can't get another bus at this time."

Eddie looked around the vehicle. It didn't look to be *that* crowded to him. "Hey, you guys mind squeezing in a little bit if it means getting to that picnic?" he asked, addressing his question to the crestfallen students.

"I don't mind," Danny spoke up.

"Me, neither," Anita called out. In short order, they were quickly joined by what sounded like the entire class.

Much as Tiffany wished the solution was that simple, there was one obvious flaw to his plan. "You can't fit all these kids in with yours on that bus," she told him. "It's just not possible."

"Not all," Eddie agreed, taking another look around the bus. "But most."

She didn't like where this seemed to be going. "How do you decide which ones don't go?" she challenged, giving him less than a minute to answer before she started telling him exactly what she thought of this "plan" of his.

"I don't," he said simply. She expected him to follow that up with "you do." But he didn't say that. What he did say was, "Because the few that can't fit on the bus can ride in my SUV."

She looked at him in surprise as her class cheered, undoubtedly ready to proclaim him a saint. He was clearly their hero.

"You drive a sedan," she reminded Eddie, raising her voice to be heard above her students.

"Not today I don't. I had to take my car in for some work, so I asked my brother-in-law if I could borrow his SUV for the day. He said okay, as long as I could deliver some equipment for him to his store at the end of the day." Eddie's dimple winked in and out as he added, "Just call it serendipity."

What she called it, albeit it just to herself, was an uncanny stroke of luck.

Or maybe a miracle.

Setting Eddie's plan in motion, the students quickly disembarked from the defunct bus and clambered onto the other one.

It turned out that all but eight students managed to squeeze into the first bus. The eight were loaded into Eddie's borrowed tan SUV.

If anyone minded being jammed into either mode of transportation, they didn't complain. The students sounded positively happy about this impromptu "adventure" they were undertaking.

"Is this what they mean by roughing it?" Danny asked her as they got under way. He was in the seat directly behind her.

"Something like that," she answered, not wanting to rob him or any of the other students of the spontaneity this field trip was generating.

Their positive attitude was severely challenged less than forty-five minutes later.

After they had arrived at the park and everyone had disembarked from the bus and the SUV, the forecast for "sunny skies" appeared to be close to becoming history. The pregnant clouds that had been hovering over them this entire time had all become dark and were looking more and more ominous by the moment.

"Now what?" one of the mothers asked Tiffany uncertainly.

"Is it going to rain on us, Mr. Montoya?" a little red-haired girl asked, looking up at Eddie. The expression on her heart-shaped face told him that she sincerely believed he could put a stop to the rain if he wanted to.

Tiffany almost expected to hear him say something to the effect of, "Not on my watch." But instead, she saw him glance up at the sky thoughtfully before saying, "Maybe, Erika. But even if it does, it's not going to rain us out,"

"You have a spell to stop the rain?" Tiffany asked in a lowered voice.

She was completely at a loss as to what Eddie could possibly do to stop this rain from hitting them. He certainly couldn't "charm" the raindrops right out of the sky, although looking around at his class, she had the impression that his students certainly seemed to think so.

"No, but I have camping tents that'll keep us dry," he announced.

Tiffany stared at him. "You're kidding, right?" But when he shook his head, she asked, "You actually brought tents?"

"No," Eddie answered honestly, already hurrying to where he had parked the vehicle he'd driven to the park. "I brought the SUV. Jake's responsible for the camping tents being in them. That's what he wanted me to drop off after school today."

Tiffany felt as if her head was spinning. Nothing was making any sense. "I don't—"

He anticipated her question and stopped her before she could tell him she wasn't following him. "My brother-in-law is co-owner of a camping gear store. Actually, it's more of a superstore," he corrected. "He runs it with his father, and he was going to be moving some of the newer tents with his SUV."

"The SUV you borrowed because your car was being worked on," Tiffany filled in.

He grinned. "Now you're catching on." He glanced up. The sky was looking very, very dark. "Tell me, how good are you at putting up tents?"

"I take directions well," she answered evasively.

Eddie grinned in approval. "That's all I wanted to know. Let's get to work," he told her, throwing open the vehicle's storage area and pulling out the boxed-up tents. "I just felt a fat raindrop on the back of my neck."

Chapter Seventeen

Within minutes of his observation, the raindrop had turned into a light shower.

Wary of what might be coming, Eddie worked at a furious pace, issuing orders and securing all the corners of the tents that he felt were necessary to shelter the picnicking students. By the time he and Tiffany, along with several of her fifth graders, had the tents up, the shower was morphing into a heavy storm.

Still issuing orders, Eddie ushered all the students, the two volunteer mothers, as well as Tiffany into the creatively connected tents before he finally took shelter there himself.

While the students and the other adults had managed to avoid getting the worst of the rain, he had not.

"Mr. Montoya, you're soaking wet," Emily, the smallest and most animated student in his class, loudly declared.

He grinned at her, touched by the concern he heard in the little girl's voice. "Fortunately, I drip-dry quickly. I'll be fine by the time we're ready to go back to school," he assured her.

As the two volunteers got the classes involved in spreading blankets and passing out packed lunches, Tiffany took him aside. Since she had nothing available that even remotely passed for a towel, she pulled off her hoodie.

"Here," she said, offering it to him.

He made no move to take it from her. "This is your sweatshirt," he protested.

She pushed it into his hands. "The rain didn't shrink my brain—I know what it is. You need something to wipe off your face and hair more than I need a piece of superficial clothing," she told him. "Besides, if it wasn't for your quick thinking and action, we'd all be as soaked as you are—and on our way back to school smelling not unlike wet sheep."

The rain was still coming down hard, pounding against the tent like angry fists. Thank heavens he'd had those tents in his vehicle, she thought.

"Someone should sue the weather bureau for breech of promise," Tiffany commented. "In no shape or form can what's outside be called a sunny sky."

Her pronouncement seemed to amuse some of the students, as well as the two mothers.

"Wouldn't do any good," Eddie told her. "The weather bureau has been getting away with inaccurate forecasts for a very long time now." He looked around at the students, who were settling in at the impromptu "indoor" picnic. "Besides, this kind of makes it a rather neat experience. Bet none of you have ever had a picnic in the rain," he said to the students.

They all took it upon themselves to answer his question, so a virtual flood of voices swarmed around him.

Eddie laughed. Then in what Tiffany was beginning to regard as his eternally calm voice, he managed to get both his class and hers to settle down somewhat.

The picnic went off without a further hitch.

In the end, it turned out to be a very unique, satisfying experience for the two classes. The sentiment was even verbalized to different degrees by several of the students.

Danny, the self-appointed leader of Tiffany's class, was the first to comment on it. There was no missing the admiration in his voice as he told the resourceful third-grade teacher, "This is the best picnic *ever*, Mr. Montoya. Anyone can have a good time when everything's going the way it's supposed to," he said sagely, just before he grinned from ear to ear. "But we got to have a great picnic in the rain."

"Sheltered *from* the rain," Anita pointed out, always needing to have the last word, especially when it meant topping Danny.

"Yeah, whatever." The boy raised his thin shoulders in a careless, dismissive shrug, sparing his class rival only the briefest of glances.

Looking in his direction, Tiffany noticed the amused look on Montoya's face. "What?" she asked, wanting to be let in on the joke.

"Nothing," he said dismissively. Then, because she continued gazing at him expectantly, he relented and shared his thoughts. "It's just that those two remind me of us, except when we were a lot older."

"I didn't sound like that," she protested.

He might have answered her, but just then his attention was hijacked by several of his third graders firing questions at him.

In the middle of that noise, Danny suddenly spoke up, his voice louder than the rest. "Hey, do you hear that?" he asked.

The boy turned his head first in one direction, then another as he posed the question, looking for all the world like a blue jay intently listening for approaching predators.

"No, I don't hear anything," Tiffany told him honestly, wondering what it was that he was hearing.

Danny's face lit up. "Yeah!" he cried. The next second he was moving quickly to where the tents had been joined together.

Eddie beat him to it and began to undo the joined flaps. "I hear you," he told the boy.

Before she could ask what they were talking about, Tiffany saw what both of them were referring to. It wasn't raining. The downpour had stopped as abruptly as it had begun.

Not only that, but as the flaps were pulled back, everyone could see that, as promised, the sun had come out.

The raindrops that had fallen on the trees were glistening like diamonds in the sun before evaporating altogether.

"The sun's out, Ms. Lee," Anita cried excitedly, clearly not wanting to be left out of the conversation. "The sun's out!"

"So I notice," she said to the girl.

"Guess the weather bureau must have overheard you saying you wanted to sue them, and pulled a few strings," Eddie joked. "No pushing!" he warned some students, who were happily pouring out of the tents on both sides of them. "Looks like they'll get their outdoor picnic, after all, so I guess this is going to turn out pretty well," he commented as the last classmates vacated the shelter.

"Oh, I don't know. I think it was going well all along," Tiffany told him. She took a deep breath. Even the smell of rain was fading. "In case you didn't notice, the kids all had a ball, thanks to your inspired camping idea." Watching as the students played, she smiled at the man beside her. The man she was beginning to believe might very well actually be flawless. "I'd say that you're officially the school hero."

Eddie shrugged away her praise, although he had to admit that it secretly pleased him. "Just used my Boy Scout training, that's all."

He actually was modest. Another admirable trait to add to the tally, Tiffany thought. "Well, you came through for them, which is all they're going to remember—even years from now."

Rather than commenting on that, Eddie glanced at his watch. "How about we give them another hour and then call them in to help take these tents down?"

Tiffany liked that he was asking her opinion rather than just telling her what the agenda was going to be. Given that he had literally saved the day for his students and hers, he had every right to dictate what they were going to do while they were out here—and yet he didn't. It made her think that maybe she needed to reevaluate everything she'd thought about him when they were in college together.

For now, she kept that to herself.

"Sounds good to me. I'll pass that along to our volunteers," she offered.

Turning away from Eddie, she circled the outer perimeter of the shelter they had put up. When she saw one of the mothers, she headed toward her to tell her the revised schedule for the outing.

As she crossed the grass, Tiffany noticed something black and wet on the ground. It was a wallet, spread open and lying facedown.

Holding it gingerly between two fingers, she searched inside for some identification. Most likely Eddie had been the one who dropped it while he was hurrying around, securing the tents so that they wouldn't suddenly blow over in the storm.

She was right. She found his driver's license tucked into the wallet, along with a couple credit cards and a bluish-looking card proclaiming him to be an organ donor.

There were no photographs in the wallet, except for one that appeared to have been folded twice over. Curious, Tiffany opened it. The creases were worn, as if the picture had been folded and unfolded countless times.

Looking at it, she saw a little boy standing a step below a little girl. He appeared to be a little older than the girl was, no more than kindergarten age, if that. The boy was carefully buttoning up the little girl's sweater while she looked on.

As she regarded the photograph, Tiffany felt something distant stir within her for just a fleeting second. And then it was gone, escaping as if it had no roots, no basis.

Most likely just her imagination. Tiffany shrugged, then hurried over to Bedford Elementary's new hero.

"You dropped this," she told him, holding out the wallet.

Eddie immediately felt his back pocket, convinced that she'd made a mistake and that his own wallet was still there.

Except it wasn't.

"Wow, you're right," he exclaimed, chagrinned. He immediately took the wallet from her. "You just saved me an awful lot of trouble," he told her. He would have had to take time off from school in order to get to the DMV to replace his driver's license, not to mention the calls he'd have to make to get his credit cards reissued. As he tucked the wallet securely back into his pocket, he asked, "Where did you find it?"

"It was lying on the ground by the far side of the tent," she replied.

"Must have fallen out when I was squatting down," he guessed.

"Must have," she parroted. She debated with herself for less than a moment before asking the question that was foremost in her mind. "Do you have kids?"

The abrupt query caught him completely off guard. "No, of course I don't have any kids. I would have told you if I did. Why?"

She wasn't finished asking her own questions yet. "A niece and nephew, then?"

He thought of his sisters. "I've got a couple of those," he admitted. But he could sense that this wasn't just some casual question on her part in lieu of small talk. "What's this all about, Tiffany?"

Her natural inclination was just to shrug and let the matter drop. But this was not "business as usual."

"Business" had stopped being usual the moment she had let him kiss her. Or, more accurately, the moment she had kissed him.

She had asked a question and he deserved to know why she'd asked—and why she wanted to know.

"When I was looking for some ID to see who the wallet belonged to, I found a photograph of a little boy and girl," she told him, waiting for him to jump in with an explanation.

But he didn't. Instead, he seemed to think that she was going to say something more about her discovery. "And?"

There was a look on Eddie's face that she couldn't begin to identify or fathom. Was he annoyed with her? Had she stumbled onto some secret he was trying to keep from surfacing?

Since he wasn't saying anything, she had no choice but to push on. "And I was just wondering if the kids were yours," she admitted.

He'd said he didn't have any, but maybe that had just been an automatic reaction. She looked at him, waiting for him to explain who the little people in the photograph were.

"Did you look at the picture closely?" Eddie asked.

What did that have to do with it? She shrugged in response. "Close enough, I guess."

"No," he told her, "I don't think so." Taking the wallet out again, he opened it and then slowly removed the photograph. Unfolding it, he held it up so she could see it. "Look closer," he instructed. "They don't seem familiar?"

What did he expect her to see? Tiffany frowned, studying the photograph. And then she suddenly remembered.

She raised her eyes to his. "I had a dress just like that when I was around four. It was a hand-me-down from one of my sisters. I hated it. I complained that it was too big and baggy, but my mother insisted I'd grow into it. I was so miserable, she compromised and bought me a sweater to put over it. I tried to hide as much of the dress as I could with it, but I could never manage to button the sweater up." Tiffany was almost hesitant as she asked, "That's me, isn't it?"

Eddie was looking at the photograph fondly and smiled as he responded. "Uh-huh."

"And you? That's you?" It was half a question, half a conclusion, as a little more of the memory whispered along the outer perimeter of her mind.

"Yes."

Despite the fragments that teased and eluded her, it still wasn't making any sense to Tiffany. "But how?"

"My mother took this picture," he told her, thinking that was what she was asking about. "She later told me that she thought we both looked so cute, with me helping you button your sweater, that she couldn't resist taking a photograph."

"We knew each other then?" Tiffany asked. But even as she did so, part of her already knew the answer to that. Faint, fragmented memories were coming back to her like ghostly apparitions. "You were the boy who held my hand and helped me cross the street to preschool," she suddenly recalled.

Eddie smiled. "You do remember, then."

The whole thing was coming back to her. "I remember that you suddenly disappeared one day, and I thought I had done something to make you go. That was you?" she asked again. "The boy in the photograph, that was you?"

"That was me."

"No," she said, shaking her head. "His name was Monty. I remember he told me that."

She'd been four at the time and it was one of her earliest memories. Back then, it seemed that the little boy who was her hero had barely moved into her neighborhood before he was gone again. After a while, despite her crush, she'd decided that she had just imagined the whole thing, including him. But now Eddie was showing her this photograph, so she couldn't have imagined it. He'd been real.

However, that still didn't change the fact that he couldn't be the boy in the photograph. But then how had he gotten it?

"I told you to call me Monty because I wanted a cool-sounding nickname and 'Eddie' didn't make the grade," he explained.

She half believed him, but she needed him to convince her. "Monty?" she questioned.

"I wanted you to like me and I thought I was being clever," he explained. "So I shortened 'Montoya' to 'Monty.'" He grinned. "What do you want, I was five."

"But where did you go?" she asked.

"My father lost his job and his uncle offered to hire him. My family had to move right away," he explained. "I wanted to tell you, but there was no time."

"Well, mystery solved," she concluded flippantly. And then she looked down at the photograph again. This time she felt a warmth filling her. "You kept this in your wallet all this time?"

Telling her that he had fallen in love with her at the age of five sounded unbelievable, so he didn't. Instead, he said, "Let's just say it was to remind me of a happier time."

Tiffany supposed she could understand that. Still, that brought up another question. "But when we ran into each other in college, why didn't you say anything at that time? Why didn't you tell me that we already knew one another?"

"You were too busy trying to get the better of me," he reminded her. Their so-called competition had flared up right from the start, at least as far as Tiffany was concerned. "If I'd said anything then, you would have thought I was trying to mess with your mind."

"I guess I was kind of competitive," she conceded.

"Kind of," he echoed with a grin.

"But you could have shown me the picture," she told him.

"Pictures can be Photoshopped."

He was right. She would have accused him of that, she thought. It struck her then that she had wasted an awful lot of time being stubborn as well as competitive. And he had put up with it all.

She felt her heart softening a little more.

The next moment, Eddie drew her attention to the vehicle behind her. "Looks like the driver's subtly trying to signal that it's time for us to get going." Eddie was back in professional mode. "I'll herd my class together. You get yours."

She nodded, glad for the distraction. She needed some time to process everything she'd just learned today.

"I can't get over the fact that you kept that photograph all these years," she said to Eddie later that evening. After the grueling day they'd put in, they had gone out for dinner. When they finished, she'd told him that she wanted to talk about her discovery somewhere private, so they went to her place.

"It's the only one I had of you, if you don't count the one that's in our graduation yearbook," Eddie told her.

That was the part she was still trying to process. "Why would you want a photograph of a woman who was always at odds with you?"

He slowly caressed her cheek, the look in his eyes saying far more than he could. "Because there was— and *is*—more to you than that. More to *us* than that when you get right down to it. And I knew that I had to just be patient until you figured that out for yourself. And when you did, I was going to show you the photograph so you could see that we really go back a long way"

Us.

It had such a nice ring to it, Tiffany thought. After all this time, after all her missteps, could she really have gotten this lucky? To have found someone to love who accepted her, faults and all? Maybe the four-year-old version of her had better instincts than she thought.

"I don't know what to say," she confessed.

"Don't say anything," Eddie told her, drawing

her into his arms. "I'm not really in the mood for a lengthy conversation right now, anyway."

There was a deliciously wicked look in his eyes, she thought, as anticipation pulsed through her veins. Her breath had lodged in her throat. "What are you in the mood for?"

He crooked his finger under her chin and raised it until her eyes met his. "Guess," he said in a low, seductive voice.

She didn't have to. Since the moment she had opened the door to admit an annoying contractor into her house, Tiffany realized that her destiny had been sealed.

"I love you, you know," she said in a throaty whisper.

"I know," he responded, a smile playing on his lips. "Oh, and I love you, too," he teased. "I always have," he told her just before he sealed his mouth to hers. The rest, he knew, would take care of itself.

And it did.

Epilogue

"It's been a long time since I've seen so many little people in one place," Maizie told her friends as she slid into the pew beside Theresa and Cilia.

"This is exactly the way the bride and groom wanted it," Theresa happily informed her two co-conspirators. "They wanted to share their big day with both of their classes."

Cilia looked around the interior of the church. The pews were filled to capacity and there were people lined up against the walls. "I'm surprised that Saint Anne's can hold so many people," she commented.

"It does seem like a tight squeeze," Maizie agreed, taking in the same scene. "What with Tiffany and Eddie each having large families, and of course their students couldn't be here without at least one parent in attendance," she noted. "Tiffany and Eddie have such big hearts, they left the invitation to both the wedding ceremony and the reception open-ended, so everyone who wanted to could attend."

Theresa chuckled softly. "Their big hearts wouldn't have done them much good if you hadn't pulled some strings to have the reception at William Mason Park." She looked at Maizie. "Do you know *everybody*?" she asked, a touch of wonder slipping into her voice.

"Pretty much," Maizie answered with surprising modesty. "In this case I thought it seemed rather fitting to have the reception in the same place that happily wound up bringing them together."

Cilia waved her hand at Maizie's words. "The park didn't bring them together, we did," she reminded her friends. "We did it by playing our parts and making sure things went smoothly."

But Maizie wasn't about to accept any undue credit, even though she'd been instrumental in making this come about, as well.

"This one was rather easy, I think. All we had to do was make sure that Eddie's name went to the top of the list so that the principal would call him to take over Mrs. Jamison's class when she went on maternity leave."

"More strings," Theresa pronounced. Tapping Maizie on the shoulder, she smiled at her with approval. "You're right," she said, winking and going along with that summation. "This one was easier than most."

"And look how happy Mei-Li is." Maizie pointed toward the woman standing in the rear of the church beside the bride. "She's marrying off the last of her daughters."

"Eddie's mother isn't exactly unhappy at the prospect of his tying the knot, either," Cilia observed, spotting the woman sitting in the front pew on the groom's side. Cilia looked at her friends on either side of her in the pew. "Ladies, I think we just keep getting better and better at this."

Maizie laughed softly. "Still, I wouldn't go quitting my day job if I were us."

Cilia laughed at the very thought. "You're never going to be quitting your day job. They'll bury you with your listings—in chronological order."

Maizie's eyes shone as she asked, "Can I help it if I like my job?"

"We *all* like our jobs," Cilia pointed out. "But that doesn't mean we can't be good at bringing happiness into people's lives."

"Amen to that," Theresa said.

"Good place to voice that sentiment," Maizie commented.

The next moment, she was waving her hand at her friends to table their conversation. The organist had started playing the wedding march.

The hush that fell over the crowd gave way to an entire churchful of people murmuring their delight at what they were witnessing. Arranged by height, with the smallest leading the way, Tiffany and Eddie's combined classes, all dressed in a charming shade of blue—the girls in frilly dresses, the boys in miniature faux-tuxedos—slowly marched down the aisle.

The procession took a while, with all the participants of the wedding party eventually filing along both sides of the altar and beyond.

And then all eyes were on the bride.

As the music swelled and grew louder, Tiffany bent her head and whispered to the small woman standing beside her, "This is it, Mom. You've been waiting your whole life to give me away and now that time's finally here. Ready?"

There were tears in Mei-Li's eyes as she stoically looked straight ahead and nodded. "Ready."

Tiffany turned her attention from her mother to the man standing at the altar.

The man waiting for her.

When she reached him, she was vaguely aware of her mother sniffling as she stepped away. Tiffany's eyes met Eddie's as her heart began hammering.

"Ready?" he asked, repeating the word she had said to her mom.

"So ready," she breathed.

"Then let's do this," he told her happily.

And they did.

* * * * *

Don't miss the next
MATCHMAKING MAMA'S *book,*
available from Harlequin Special Edition
in July 2017!

And catch up on the miniseries
with these previous titles:

TWICE A HERO, ALWAYS HER MAN
DR. FORGET-ME-NOT
COMING HOME FOR CHRISTMAS
HER RED-CARPET ROMANCE

Available now wherever Harlequin Special Edition
books and ebooks are sold!

Dear Reader,

This month—April 2017—marks the 35th anniversary for Harlequin Special Edition! Perhaps it's as hard for you, the reader, to believe this as it is for us, the team that has been presenting this warm, wonderful and relatable series of books for all these years. And while some of us are newer than others, the one thing that has always been consistent is that the Harlequin Special Edition lineup has always reached out and grabbed you, made you want to read more, made you look forward to what comes next.

April 2017 is a great illustration of this. We have *New York Times* bestselling author Brenda Novak in Harlequin Special Edition for the first time with *Finding Our Forever*, alongside our almost-brand-new author Katie Meyer with another in her Proposals in Paradise series, *The Groom's Little Girls*. We have *USA TODAY* bestselling and beloved authors Marie Ferrarella (*Meant to be Married*) and Judy Duarte in our next Fortunes of Texas: The Secret Fortunes story (*From Fortune to Family Man*). And if it's glamour, glitz and sparkle you want with your romance, look no further than *The Princess Problem* (next in the Drake Diamonds trilogy) by Teri Wilson.

We have moved through the last thirty-five years giving you, the reader, stories that warmed your heart and curled your toes, and we are just getting started! So happy anniversary...and here's to the next thirty-five!

Happy Reading,

Gail Chasan
Senior Editor, Harlequin Special Edition

COMING NEXT MONTH FROM

H HARLEQUIN®

SPECIAL EDITION

Available April 18, 2017

#2545 THE LAWMAN'S CONVENIENT BRIDE
The Bravos of Justice Creek • by Christine Rimmer
Jody Bravo has vowed to raise her baby alone and do it right. But Sheriff Seth Yancy, whose deceased stepbrother is the father of Jody's child, is going to protect and look after the baby and Jody—whether she wants his help or not.

#2546 CHARM SCHOOL FOR COWBOYS
Hurley's Homestyle Kitchen • by Meg Maxwell
When pregnant Emma Hurley starts a charm school for rancher Jake Morrow's lovelorn cowboys, she never expected to enter into a fake engagement with Jake. But when her father threatens to sell her family farm, Emma will do whatever it takes to save it, even risk her heart!

#2547 HER KIND OF DOCTOR
Men of the West • by Stella Bagwell
Nurse Paige Winters and Dr. Luke Sherman have butted heads since they started working in the ER together. But after she finally gives him a piece of her mind and switches floors, Luke realizes Paige is much more than just another nurse, and he's determined to prove he's exactly her kind of doctor!

#2548 FORTUNE'S SURPRISE ENGAGEMENT
The Fortunes of Texas: The Secret Fortunes
by Nancy Robards Thompson
Olivia Fortune Robinson has to prove to her sister that love is real, stat! So she convinces everyone that she and Alejandro Mendoza are madly in love. And when he proposes, she's just as shocked as everyone else. But his past loss and her present cynicism threaten to keep this surprise engagement from becoming the real thing.

#2549 THE LAST SINGLE GARRETT
Those Engaging Garretts! • by Brenda Harlen
When Josh Slater finds himself entrusted with the care of his three nieces for the summer, he's forced to rely on his best friend's younger sister, Tristyn Garrett, for help. But their attraction has simmered below the surface for twelve years, and a summer spent on an RV road trip looks to be their breaking point...

#2550 THE BRONC RIDER'S BABY
Rocking Chair Rodeo • by Judy Duarte
Former rodeo cowboy Nate Gallagher has just discovered he's the daddy of a newborn baby girl—and starts falling for Anna Reynolds, the pretty social worker assigned to assess whether he's true father material! Nate knows the stakes are higher than ever. He's not just risking his heart, but a future for his daughter.

YOU CAN FIND MORE INFORMATION ON UPCOMING HARLEQUIN® TITLES, FREE EXCERPTS AND MORE AT WWW.HARLEQUIN.COM.

HSECNM0417

"Mirabelle's?" It was a new restaurant in town, a small, cozy place with white tablecloths and crystal chandeliers and a chef from New York. Everyone said the food was really good and the service impeccable.

"I heard it was good," he said. "Would you rather go somewhere else?"

"I just didn't know we were doing that."

"Doing what?"

"Going through with the date."

He set down his fork. "We're doing it." His voice was deep and rough, and his velvet-brown gaze caught hers and held it.

It just wasn't fair that the guy was so damn hot. *Not happening*, she reminded herself. *Don't get ideas.* "What about Marybeth?"

"It's only a few hours. Get a sitter. Maybe one of your sisters or maybe your mom?"

"Ma? Please."

"She did raise five children, didn't she?"

"She's probably off on her next cruise already."

"A babysitter, Jody. I'm sure you can find one."

"But Marybeth is barely four weeks old."

"Jody. We're going. Stop making excuses."

She sagged back in her chair. "Why are you so determined about this?"

"Because I want to take you out."

"But…you don't go out, remember? There's no point because it can't go anywhere. Not to mention, I live in Broomtail County, and what if it got messy with me?"

"Too late." He was almost smiling. She could see that increasingly familiar twitch at the corner of his mouth. "It's already messy with you."

"I am not joking, Seth."

"Neither am I. I want to be with you, Jody. And not just as a friend."

"B-but I…" God. She was sputtering. And why did she suddenly feel light as a breath of air, as if she was floating on moonbeams? "You want to be with me? But you don't do that. You've made that very clear."

"You're right. I didn't do that. Until now. But things have changed."

"Because of Marybeth, you mean?"

"Yeah, because of Marybeth. And because of you, too. Because of the way you are. Strong and honest and smart and so pretty. Because we've got something going on, you and me. Something good. I'm through pretending that we're friends and nothing more. Are you telling me I'm the only one who feels that way?"

"I just…" Her pulse raced and her cheeks felt too hot. She'd promised herself that nothing like this would happen, that she wouldn't get her hopes up.

She needed to be careful. She could end up with her heart in pieces all over again.

Don't miss
THE LAWMAN'S CONVENIENT BRIDE
by Christine Rimmer, available May 2017 wherever
Harlequin® Special Edition books and ebooks are sold.

www.Harlequin.com

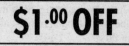

$1.⁰⁰ OFF

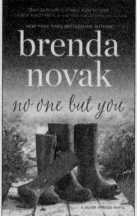

"Brenda Novak is always a joy to read."
DEBBIE MACOMBER, #1 new york times bestselling author

NEW YORK TIMES BESTSELLING AUTHOR

brenda novak

no one but you

A SILVER SPRINGS NOVEL

$7.99 U.S./$9.99 CAN.

New York Times
bestselling author
brenda novak

welcomes you to Silver
Springs, a picturesque small
town in Southern California
where even the hardest hearts
can learn to love again…

MIRA®

Available May 30, 2017.

$1.⁰⁰ OFF

the purchase price of NO ONE BUT YOU
by Brenda Novak.

Offer valid from May 30, 2017, to June 30, 2017.
Redeemable at participating retail outlets, in-store only. Not redeemable at
Barnes & Noble. Limit one coupon per purchase. Valid in the U.S.A. and Canada only.

52614662

5 65373 00076 2 (8100)0 12267

® and ™ are trademarks owned and used by the trademark owner and/or its licensee.

© 2017 Harlequin Enterprises Limited

MCOUPBN0617

THE WORLD IS BETTER WITH

Romance

Harlequin has everything from contemporary, passionate and heartwarming to suspenseful and inspirational stories.

Whatever your mood, we have a romance just for you!

Connect with us to find your next great read, special offers and more.

 /HarlequinBooks

@HarlequinBooks

www.HarlequinBlog.com

www.Harlequin.com/Newsletters

HARLEQUIN®

A *Romance* FOR EVERY MOOD™

www.Harlequin.com